Christmas Without You

JULIA AMANTE

WISE WRITER PUBLISHING

Amante, Julia, 1967-

Christmas Without You / Julia Amante - First edition 2024

ISBN: 978-1931627122

     1. Second Chance Romance – Fiction

     2. Romance Paranormal – Fiction

     3. Christmas – Fiction

     4. South Dakota/ Mid-west/ Black Hills

Book Cover by The Killion Group Inc.

Dedicated to all those who believe true love is heaven-sent.

And to my children: may they always believe in the magic of life!

Contents

CHAPTER ONE

J aden disentangled himself from the embrace of an emotional, clingy, and beautifully naked woman.

"But Christmas is three weeks away." She pouted, wrapping her arms tightly around his waist and pulling him back into the bubbling hot tub when he stood to get out. "Stay with me." Sliding down his body, she licked the ridges of his abs.

"Mmm," he said, looking down at the moist curls on top of her head, feeling tempted to stay. The outdoor lights in her backyard made the droplets of water on her wet skin shimmer like tiny diamonds. But he gently gripped her shoulders and eased her back. Before she could reach for him again, he sprung out of the tub and grabbed a towel, wrapping it around his waist.

"Jaden, this is ridiculous. No one is working this close to Christmas, and they are especially not buying collectible cars. I don't understand why you have to leave."

"Christmas is the perfect time for people with money to invest in luxury vehicles. Clients are blowing up my phone every day." He winked. "So, I have to go."

"Will you be back for Christmas?" she asked, resting her chin on her folded arms, watching him as he dried off.

He was probably quite a sight. The December air in Colorado was biting cold. As he emerged from the warmth of the hot tub, the contrast was clearly visible—his body radiating heat, the cold air transforming it into a swirling mist. Steam rose from his skin, and every breath he exhaled seemed to turn to vapor instantly.

She waited for an answer, so he shook his head. This relationship had run its course. "No." He held up a hand as she began to protest. "I will send you a Christmas gift that you will love, but I can't be here for Christmas."

She narrowed her eyes. "A gift? Will it fit on my finger?"

Not on your life. "It's not that kind of surprise." He'd bought her a sexy dress she'd admired recently when they strolled through a mall. The store would deliver her gift next week. He hurried inside her house to her bedroom, where he dressed in black slacks and a white button-down shirt. His usual. He'd shower later.

She strolled in, still naked, her skin flushed from the heat of the water. She sat on the bed, dropping down on her side, stretching her legs out seductively, and holding her head with her hand. "Jaden, am I going to see you again?"

They'd been together about five months. They met at a birthday party he attended last summer in honor of one of his Denver clients. Jaden sighed. "Why would you ask that?"

"You're distant. You don't want to spend time with me. What did I do wrong?"

He reached down and placed a hand on her cheek. "Nothing. You're great. I'm just...I have to work." He grabbed his coat. "I'll call you. Okay?"

"Yeah," she said. "Merry Christmas, Jaden."

Jaden didn't run, but he made a hasty retreat, that's for sure. Messy relationships and clingy women seemed to be the only kind who found him. Relationships. They weren't for him. One day, he was all into a woman, and the next, it was all he could do to focus on what they were saying. Something was wrong with him. He was the common denominator here. The women were all lovely.

He got into the Jaguar coupe he'd rented for the weekend and stepped on it. He drove on the icy roads, feeling better as the miles took him further and further away from her very nice ranch house in Elizabeth, Colorado. He reached across to the passenger seat, reaching for a gift from a business associate—a bottle of peanut butter whiskey.

"Oh yeah," he said. He wanted to open the bottle right now and take a big swig. And he planned to do just that when he got to the airport since unfortunately, he wouldn't be able to take it with him on the plane. "Whoo!" The odometer moved from 95 to 100 to 110. Life was good. He felt like he was flying. Fast cars. An empty road. Freedom. That's what life was about.

In the darkness, trees, random farmhouses, and cows were a blur as he zoomed past them all. He didn't exactly see the object that appeared like a blip on the road. But he felt the solid impact that sent his car tumbling. The back end lifted, and the car flipped front to back three times before stopping.

A shock of pain ran through his body, causing everything to go black for a moment. Jaden moaned and tried to clear the dizziness in his head. He opened his eyes and tried to make sense of his surroundings. Flashing lights surrounded his car, and he heard people talking frantically. Jaden climbed out of the car through the window, and in typical dream-like fashion, the scene had changed, and he was no longer outside by the side of the dark road. Instead, he found himself in a bright lobby that resembled a hospital waiting room.

"Jaden?" A young guy with curly blond hair and white scrubs stood beside him.

"Ah, yeah. Where am I?" He looked around the large room without doors or windows. "What happened to my car?"

"I'm Ben. Your car was totaled. A tow truck took it away."

Jaden looked down at his clothes. His slacks were torn, and his favorite Luca Faloni shirt was filthy with dirt and bloodstains. He still wore his suit coat. Shit. "Am I in a hospital?" Had he passed out?

"No, Jaden. Not anymore."

Jaden ran a hand through his hair, scratching the back of his head and feeling a slight bump. "Can I sit down? I'm really confused."

"Of course." Ben pointed to a row of chairs up against a white wall. "It's normal to be confused. The transition can be difficult."

Jaden frowned. The room suddenly felt cool and too quiet. "Transition?"

"You didn't make it out of the car crash alive, I'm afraid.

Jaden laughed. "Are you telling me I'm dead?"

Ben just stared at Jaden without any expression, as if letting it sink in.

"I'm dreaming, right? I fell asleep on her bed after I got out of the hot tub." Jaden slapped his face to try to wake up.

"You're not dreaming. You shouldn't drink and drive, by the way."

What?" Jaden pointed at Ben's face. "Hey, I didn't."

"No, but you wanted to. And you took your eyes off the road and were driving recklessly. You hit that deer at 115 miles per hour. Neither one of you had a chance."

"A deer? Crap, it felt like a rock." Jaden stood, gazing around the room. For the first time, he noticed a few people who walked around the nearly empty lobby, talking, crying, in shock, like him. "Am I in heaven?"

"No."

Jaden took a tentative step toward Ben. "Hell?" He raked his brain, trying to remember what he had done wrong. "I wasn't that bad, was I?"

Ben's calm smile eased his anxiety. "It's a waiting area."

"Waiting for what? I've got to get the hell out of here. I mean, not hell. You know what I mean. I'm leaving."

"You can't. There are no exits. Just relax, Jaden."

He spoke soothingly, like the British broadcaster David Attenborough. Calmly. He even had a bit of a British accent. Jaden had watched some of the BBC nature show documentaries that he had narrated. But this guy wasn't Attenborough, and he irritated the shit out of him. "I don't know you. I thought when you died, you got to see your family. Why isn't my mom or dad or grandma here to greet me?"

"In time," Ben reassured him. His eyes fixed on Jaden with a curious intensity. "Tell me, Jaden. Do you like women?"

Jaden raised his eyebrows in surprise at the sudden change of topic. He hesitated for a moment before answering cautiously, not sure where this was going. "Of course," he finally replied, trying to read Ben's expression.

"Then why did you always run away from them?" Ben pressed further, his tone still gentle as if trying to understand something beyond his comprehension.

Jaden tensed momentarily, and then he laughed. "I didn't run away."

"You did." Ben's voice was firm, as if there was no room for argument; it was simply a fact.

Jaden shook his head and stood. He walked around the lobby, which was devoid of furniture except for the chairs, looking for a door. But the room seemed to stretch as he walked. He never reached the other side, and when he turned back around, Ben and the chairs were right behind him as if he hadn't walked away at all. This was starting to scare him. He took a seat again and held his head in his hands.

"Do you know you've ruined Christmas for every woman you've ever met?" Ben asked.

Jaden dropped his hands, and his eyes widened slightly. "I ruined Christmas? Are you joking?"

Screens suddenly appeared. They didn't drop down, but they were just there as if they'd been there all along. Five huge flat-screen TVs. And they started playing Christmas scenes. From his life! Stephanie, crying when he broke up with her on Christmas Eve over the phone. Rachel, slapping him when he showed up drunk at her house on another Christmas Eve when he was supposed to meet her family. Kim, tossing him out in the snow; Caroline, yelling at him; Andrea, walking away from his warehouse as he stood by his cars where he'd told her it was over. Christmas after Christmas, ten of them, all in reverse, ending with Keri, his high school sweetheart, sitting alone on the bench in the park by the high school where he'd proposed. It was Christmas morning, a few days after he left. He'd never said goodbye.

Ben cleared his throat. "No joke. You ruined all their Christmases."

Jaden felt like shit. "I guess I did." He turned to Ben. "So, I'm going to hell. I deserve it."

"No." Ben laughed. "Oh, hold on a second." He tilted his head as if he were listening to a bird in a tree. Then he nodded and made a note on his iPad, but it wasn't an iPad; it was translucent and glowed. "So, Jaden, I have good news. How would you like to make this right?"

"Make what right?"

"What if I gave you an opportunity to choose one of these women? To go back and give them an unforgettable Christmas."

"What, like go back and have a redo? Relive the Christmas when I left them?"

"No, you're not a time traveler. You can't go back to an earlier time. But you can give one of these ladies an incredible Christmas *this* year. You'll have to figure out how. We can't help you with that."

"And if I can't?"

Ben just shrugged. "Then I'll see you again."

Jaden was even more confused and tired. "Yeah, sure."

Ben brightened. "Excellent! This will be fun."

Gazing at the young guy, Jaden smirked. Glad he was so happy about this.

"You have three weeks. You won't remember me. You won't remember this at all." He looked at the tablet and made a note. "That's just the way it works. Which woman?"

"Oh, I don't care." He rubbed the back of his head and glanced up at the screens again. "Wait, actually, make it her." He pointed to Keri. He'd loved her once. At least, he thought it was love. He was so young; what did he know?

"Okay," Ben said. "Perfect choice. Now, Jaden, this is going to hurt just a little."

"Hurt?" And suddenly, he was on a gurney; his side ached, and his head felt like it had been stepped on by a herd of deer.

"It's okay," a nurse said while making notes on a chart. "I'll get you more painkillers in a second."

"Where? I mean, I was just talking to . . . "

"To whom? No one has been in to see you except the doctor."

"Yeah, I . . . don't know. I don't know what I was going to say. What am I doing here?"

"You were in an accident, Mr. Lowe. We thought we'd lost you. You came in with so many injuries, but . . . they disappeared." She chuckled. "Of course, they can't disappear. I guess they weren't as bad as we originally thought. Miraculously, you're fine. Your ribs are bruised. And you have a bit of a concussion. By morning, you'll feel much better."

"Okay." He closed his eyes and leaned back. But she told him he had to stay awake. Damn, he felt like hell.

No one had been in to see him? He thought for a second and remembered that he'd been driving toward Denver, headed to the airport. Who would come to see him? No one knew where he was. Not that anyone would be looking for him. Jaden was all alone. And that was how he liked it, wasn't it?

Although the nurse told him to stay awake, his eyes closed. He needed to rest, and then he had things to do. But he couldn't remember what. "It's something important," he mumbled. "I only have three weeks."

The pounding in his head didn't allow him to think, but an image of a pretty girl floated behind his eyelids...his high school sweetheart. And he relaxed.

CHAPTER TWO

K eri's slender fingers turned the wooden sign on the door of her small art store from open to closed.

The sun was setting behind the Black Hills, casting a warm orange glow on the quaint storefront. She'd opened her business in Custer almost six years ago when she graduated from college with a degree in business and decided the most important thing she'd learned about business was that she didn't want to work in a big city for a large company. However, owning her own place and working for herself appealed to her.

She took a risk and created an artist cooperative for all local artists to sell their creative works to tourists who visited the Black Hills. Her artistic contributions to the store were wine racks she made out of horseshoes she collected from her brother's ranch. When she first started creating these bizarre creations, they looked horrible and tacky, but after years of working with them, they had become novelty pieces that people seemed to love.

She also sold jewelry, wood carvings, birdhouses, paintings, lovely photos of the local area, quilts, and even cool greeting cards that local artists dropped off weekly for Keri to sell.

With less than three weeks to go until Christmas, she'd been busy displaying and selling mostly Christmas items her artist friends created for the season. With their help, her store turned into a magical Christmas haven. She'd placed two large Christmas trees, one in each corner of the store, and filled them with uniquely created ornaments that customers loved. As soon as she stepped into the store each day, Keri was greeted with the inviting scent of the pine trees, mixed with the sweet smell of cinnamon and spices from the scented candles she had strategically placed throughout the store.

In the glass cases were snowmen, Santas, elves, reindeer, Christmas trees, and little village houses. A couple of her jewelry makers brought her Christmas-themed rings, necklaces, and bracelets. Coming to work felt like being enclosed in Santa's workshop at the North Pole, but instead of being surrounded by toys, she was enveloped by festive and inspiring art.

Not for the first time, she sent a silent thank you to the heavens above for allowing her to make a living doing what she loved. But tonight, the area was expecting snow, and she was closing early.

Her small apartment in Rapid City would be warm and welcoming. A bowl of soup, a good book, some thick socks, and a blanket awaited her—a perfect night. But her phone rang on the drive home, pulling her out of her thoughts. She activated the hands-free feature in her truck and responded to the call.

"Keri, we're going Christmas tree shopping," her friend Samantha's voice came through the speakers. "Are you still at work?"

"I'm on my way home, Sam."

"Great! Do you want to meet us at the lot or stop by my house and go together?"

Since high school, she and her friends had shopped for their Christmas trees together. As the old gang had gotten married and had kids, their families had tagged along, and it had become "a thing," and Keri loved it, but not tonight. "It's going to snow."

"Even better!"

She groaned. So much for her quiet evening.

"Come on. Amber's sick kids made us cancel last weekend. Let's do this. Or it's going to be Christmas Eve, and I still won't have a tree. My twins ask me every day when we're going to get our tree."

"Yeah, I haven't put any decorations up myself. My house lacks Christmas spirit. Do you have food? I'm starving."

"I'll make you a sandwich. Come over."

"On my way."

In the morning, Jaden checked himself out of the hospital and called an Uber to take him to the airport. While he waited for his flight home to Los Angeles, he bought a coffee and a breakfast sandwich. He'd have to call the insurance company to let them know about his rental car. They were not going to be happy.

As he stared at the flights and cities on the flight board, he saw Rapid City, his hometown, and had a sudden urge to go back home. He hadn't been back in ten years.

No one has been in to see you. The nurse's words came back to him. That's because he had no one, no family, except one uncle. His parents died when he was a kid. They were vacationing in Thailand for Christmas when a tsunami struck the day after Christmas. They'd left Jaden with his uncle, and he'd been thrilled. His uncle, his mother's brother, was always a lot of fun and to him, spending Christmas with Uncle Frank instead of in a foreign country with his parents had been a million times better. And lucky for him. His parents were among the 250,000 people killed that day. Uncle Frank became his legal guardian overnight. Jaden missed his uncle.

Impulsively, he stood and went back to the gate to change his flight. Why not? He had no reason to return to Los Angeles right away, and spending Christmas with his uncle after so many years was exactly what he needed.

As he sat in his first-class seat drinking lukewarm coffee, he wondered what had gotten into him. Why this urge to head back home? Maybe almost dying got a guy thinking about seeing family. His uncle was the only family he had; he didn't have brothers or sisters, and Uncle Frank never got married or had kids, so no cousins either. It had been the two of them for years. Well, the two of them and Uncle Frank's girlfriend of the month.

The randomness of life had always struck Jaden as unfair, but it had taught him not to trust that anything would stay the same. So, he took advantage of whatever opportunities came his way and enjoyed them while they lasted.

Spending Christmas with his uncle sounded perfect. He'd relax. Heal his bruised ribs and cuts. Drink and laugh with the old man. And then, he'd be good as new and ready to tackle his work in the new year.

He slept through most of the flight, then rented a boring white Nissan and drove the short distance to his uncle's house.

Uncle Frank's house was small and cozy, with a wrap-around porch decorated with twinkling Christmas lights. Through the windows, he could see a warm fire crackling in the fireplace and smell the smoky scent in the air. Jaden found his uncle on the porch carrying a puny little tree into his house.

"Hey, couldn't you afford a real tree?"

Uncle Frank stopped struggling with the tree and looked over his shoulder. "What the hell? What are you doing here?"

Jaden stepped forward, his hands in his suit coat. He needed a jacket. "Freezing. Let me inside." He took the tree out of Frank's hands and pulled it inside. "Seriously, what is this, a bush?"

"It's a damn tree. I don't need anything bigger; it's just me." He stared at Jaden's face, then grinned. "Get in a fight?"

"A car crash. I don't look too bad, do I?"

"You don't look too good. But I'm happy to see you." He patted Jaden's back and shoulders. "Staying long?"

"Until Christmas or the New Year, maybe, if that's okay with you. I can get a hotel, but—."

"Nonsense. Why would you go to a hotel when I have empty rooms?" He looked Jaden up and down one more time, then turned away.

He walked slower than the last time Jaden had seen him. Although Jaden called home, he didn't visit.

Uncle Frank took a seat in his brown leather recliner. "You got bags?"

"Nope, I had an overnight bag, but I think it got lost in the accident. I decided to visit at the last minute."

"Of course, you did," Uncle Frank said, as if not surprised.

"How have you been Uncle Frank? We haven't talked since . . . shit, last Christmas?"

"Getting older. Making all the old ladies at the senior center happy." He raised and lowered his eyebrows suggestively, looking like a creepy lecher.

Jaden laughed. "I'll bet. Good ole Uncle Frank."

He slid his hands up and down his legs as if they hurt, but he smiled. "I'm not dead yet."

"No, you're not. That's a good thing. You got food?"

"Not really. Some frozen food in the freezer."

Jaden glanced at his tree. "What do you say I go get you a real tree and some pizza and beer?"

"I have beer."

"All right then. I'll get the tree and the pizza."

"My tree is fine. Why are you obsessing over a stupid tree?"

Jaden shrugged. "Maybe I want the place to look like it did when I was a kid. Remember when you'd let me choose the biggest tree I could find?"

"As long as—."

"It fits in the den, Boy." Jaden finished the sentence that his uncle had said for years.

Uncle Frank appeared to get tears in his eyes. Was he getting emotional in his old age? "Right," he said. "Well, if you're going to go get that pizza and a bigger tree, go do it before I fall asleep."

Jaden nodded. Even as sore and tired as he was, going to pick out a Christmas tree excited him, made him feel like . . . he was home.

"Can I take your jacket? I don't have any clothes except what I'm wearing."

"There's extra coats and gloves in the closet. Take what you need." He reached for the TV remote and settled into his chair.

Jaden picked out a coat. "I'll be back soon."

The frosty air was filled with the smell of pine and fresh snow. As they passed by different trees, the scent of cedar and spruce mixed in, helping Keri get into the spirit of Christmas tree shopping. Keri, her three friends, their seven children, and only one husband strolled along the dirt path looking for the perfect trees.

Amanda's kids, who had been bouncing with excitement from the moment they arrived, were the first to find a ten-footer they absolutely had to have. Jenn's husband, Paul, helped to cut it down. Then the lot workers netted the monster of a tree and placed it in the back of her pickup.

Inspired, Jenn's two kids were the next to choose a tree, but Paul shook his head when he saw what they were pointing to. "We can't have such a big tree, guys. Try to find a seven- or eight-foot max."

They groaned but quickly began their search for the right size tree, scampering away with the other kids, promising they'd find the best tree left on the lot.

Happy Christmas music blared through the speakers. Keri smiled. "Must be nice to have a family to celebrate Christmas with."

"What, your parents, brother, and your nieces and nephews aren't family anymore?" Samantha asked.

"You know what I mean. A husband and kids."

Sam sighed. "You could have mine. I'm tired of them."

Keri laughed. She had adorable five-year-old twin boys. Her husband worked at Ellsworth Air Force Base, so he was gone a lot, but she still had someone who loved her to death. "You wouldn't trade them for a million dollars," Keri said.

"Oh, I don't know. Some days, I'd trade them for a weekend retreat somewhere hot and sunny where they serve you fruity drinks."

Looking up at the tiny snowflakes that were beginning to come down, she nodded. "That sounds good right about now. I'd better find my tree quickly."

After an hour, they'd all found their trees except Keri. She didn't want anything too big since it was just her in the small apartment. She looked at the three-foot trees, but the kids told her she had to go at least five feet, or it didn't count.

She strolled beside an impressive noble fir that was indeed about five feet. "Okay, this one," she said just as another guy wearing reindeer antlers pointed at the tree and told the kid with a saw to cut her tree down.

"No," the kids sang.

The man turned, taking in the pack of kids, then he glanced at her. "Oh, did you guys want this one?"

Keri frowned. Was that...? No, couldn't be.

"I could choose another one if your kids want . . ." He angled his head and seemed to recognize her, but he didn't say anything. He turned back to the attendant. "I'll keep looking. You can cut this one down for the kids."

Still staring at him as he turned away, Keri tuned out the kids' cheering. After the tree was cut, they picked it up on their own and carried it to be netted.

"Jaden?" she said, not even noticing that she'd walked toward him as he inspected the nearby trees. Snow fell lightly, making him appear dreamlike.

He raised an eyebrow, focusing on her almost reluctantly. "You're welcome," he said.

"What?"

"The tree." He pointed to where the tree had been.

"That's all you're going to say? Are you going to pretend you don't know who I am? I haven't changed that much."

With a sexy, slow grin, he nodded. "I know who you are, even if you are buried under that heavy coat and cute hat. How have you been, Keri?"

How had she been? Her son-of-a-bitch fiancé walked out on her without saying a word ten years ago, and all he had to say now was, 'How have you been?'

"I've been fantastic," she replied sarcastically. "What are you doing here?"

"Getting a tree." He gestured toward the rows of evergreens behind him. At the look on her face, he laughed. "Oh, you mean in town? Spending Christmas with Uncle Frank. In fact, I'm getting him a proper tree. He had this embarrassing little thing that couldn't really be considered a tree."

Keri stared at him, emotions swirling inside her like a whirlwind. Of all the times she'd thought of seeing him again, never once did she imagine it would be having a casual conversation in a Christmas tree lot. "Well, wish your uncle a Merry Christmas. I'm sure he's happy to see you."

As she turned to leave, he called after her, "Hey, maybe we can get together while I'm here."

"Seriously?"

"Oh, sorry. You must be married, considering you're here with all those kids."

Samantha's voice came from behind Keri, startling her. "You think she managed to pop out seven kids between the ages of five and eight?"

He glanced over Keri's shoulder and, for the first time, noticed her friends all watching the exchange in rapt attention.

"Hi, Samantha." He greeted her full of forced excitement before turning back to Keri with a smile. "They're not all yours. Of course."

"I'll pass on getting together."

"You sure? We can have a drink. Catch up?"

She stared at the guy she'd once loved so deeply, disappointed that he could be so heartless. "Did it ever occur to you to let me know you were leaving ten years ago? To call me. To explain. Anything?"

Finally, his stupid grin disappeared, a flicker of guilt replacing the amusement on his face.

"I called you and went to your house," Keri continued. "I was worried and confused. I didn't know what had happened to you."

"I should have said something." Jaden agreed.

"You're an asshole," she said. She had nothing else to say to him after all these years. It didn't matter anymore. She'd cried for months. Spent years getting over him, secretly waiting for him to return. But that was so long ago that she couldn't remember why she cared so much.

She left him standing there, about to say something else, looking ridiculous in reindeer antlers.

"Are you okay?" Sam asked when they all reached her truck.

"Fine. It was a shock to see him, but I'm glad I finally got to tell him what I think of him."

"You should have punched him. Though it looked like someone already did." Amanda said.

"Why would I waste any energy on that loser?" She hugged Sam and the rest of her friends. "I'm going to go home and put my tree up, have a cup of hot chocolate, and enjoy the rest of the night, grateful that I didn't end up with that prick."

"He's still just as clueless as he was in high school," Sam said.

"Yeah," Jenn said. "Clueless and self-centered."

"And obviously still alone. The loser," Amber added.

Keri laughed. She was lucky to have wonderful friends on her side when the guy who broke her heart didn't even seem to realize how much pain he'd caused.

A quick glance in his direction verified that he was gone, not giving her a second thought. Vanished just like ten years ago.

CHAPTER THREE

With a slight struggle and an achy side, Jaden carried the five-foot tree into Uncle Frank's living room. The tree stand was already waiting for him in front of a large window with a view of Frank's large front yard, so Jaden cut the netting and plopped the tree where he was instructed. He got the tree straight, then stood back to make sure it looked good.

"Decorations are in the garage," Frank said.

"Hold on a sec." He ran back to his car to get the pizza, which was probably cold. Even cold, pizza was delicious.

Jaden placed the box on the coffee table and sat on the couch. "You mind if we decorate the tree in the morning? I'm beat."

"I would have been decorated if you hadn't insisted on getting a different tree. What am I supposed to do with the one I bought? I paid ten bucks for it, you know." He winced as he stood and went to the kitchen to get the beer.

"I'll go get the decorations box." With a resigned sigh, Jaden pushed himself up off the couch. "And I'll give you the ten bucks."

"No, no. Sit down." He handed Jaden a Coors Light. "Tell me what you've been up to. And why do you have those stupid reindeer antlers on?"

Jaden dropped back down, taking the prop off his head. "The cute girl at the counter of the Christmas tree lot told me I'd look cute in them, so I bought them."

"She lied."

Jaden nodded, figuring as much. But he'd been having fun. He popped the beer open and took a drink. Ugh, this was terrible. He had to buy his uncle better beer. "I haven't been doing much. Working. Making money. Keeping busy."

"The last time you called was two years ago, you know. Not last year."

"I'm sorry." He offered an honest apology. He'd already been called an asshole once tonight. "I lose track of time. I thought I called you last year."

Uncle Frank rolled his eyes, a familiar gesture that reminded Jaden of his youth when he'd done something dumb and should have known better.

"I thought maybe you got married and were busy running after kids."

Jaden winced as he rubbed his aching ribs. Sitting down was more painful than standing. "That would require me to settle down, and we both know that's never going to happen."

"You wanna end up like your old uncle, huh?" He pulled up a greasy slice of pepperoni pizza and put half of it in his mouth.

"Not a bad life." Jaden grinned. "Never heard you complaining."

"No complaints. But . . . you know. I had you. If I hadn't, I might have ended up a lonely, grumpy middle-aged man with no one to share my life with. You filled a void. Know what I'm sayin', boy?"

Jaden's uncle never lacked female companionship. Some woman was always willing to share her life with him. By being inconsiderate or just plain difficult, he was the one who always chased women away.

Jaden finished a slice of pizza and reached for a second.

"You listening to me?" Frank asked.

"I am. Are you saying you would have gotten married if you hadn't had me?" Jaden often felt like he was in the way. When he was old enough, he'd stay gone, usually to Keri's house. She had the perfect parents, and they always made him feel welcome. Plus, they loved him, and it felt good to be cared for.

"No, I'm saying I wasn't lonely because I had you. But you have no one."

"I like it that way." Jaden winked and downed the rest of his beer, and took the last few bites. But he had to admit that seeing Keri tonight felt like a sock to the stomach. She looked adorable with her rosy cheeks, wearing a little hat with a fuzzy ball on top, surrounded by kids. For just a second, he wasn't sure if it was her, and as soon as he realized it was, he tried to get away as fast as possible because he didn't want to think about what he'd give up.

"Listen, I'm going to take some painkillers and go to sleep. It's good to see you, Uncle Frank. You look good. We'll talk more and decorate that tree in the morning, okay?"

"Sure. Get some rest. You know where your old room is. A woman redecorated it for me, but I told her to leave your stuff in there."

Jaden walked into his childhood room, took off all his clothes except his boxers, pulled the sheets and blankets back, and carefully got into bed. He moaned; this felt like heaven. He needed to get back up to wash his face, brush his teeth, and turn out the light, but not yet. He was so tired, and his body ached. Being back here hurt, too. There were so many memories — mostly good ones. Some sad. He opened his eyes, lifted his head, and took in the room. Some woman decorated it, Uncle Frank said. She'd taken Jaden's photos that he'd left behind in drawers, framed them, and plastered one of his walls as a memorial to his past. Looking back at him were pictures of his friends, and there was Keri, a photo he'd taken of her on a hike.

He struggled to get out of bed and pulled the picture off the wall. Sexy and sweet. He'd loved this picture. She'd been resting on her belly on the grass with the lake and trees as a backdrop. He'd called her name, and she'd lifted her head, turned to her side just a little, one arm in front of her, and another behind, holding her head. She'd gazed at him with so much love and desire. He'd snapped a few pictures, thinking she was the most beautiful woman in the world.

But what he saw now in the picture was a girl, not a woman—innocent, beautiful, young. He placed the photo on a dresser.

Tonight, he'd seen a woman. And she definitely didn't look at him the same way.

The next morning, after sharing a full breakfast of eggs, sausage, and toast with his uncle, Jaden asked Frank about Keri. Where she lived. Where she worked. If she was married. Something inside made him want to find her and talk to her properly. He hadn't reacted well last night. Trying to play it light and friendly probably hadn't been smart.

"Why do you ask?"

"I ran into her last night at the Christmas tree lot. She called me an asshole and left." He mopped up the egg yolk with his bread.

Uncle Frank chuckled. "Well, she's not wrong. Maybe that should be a clue to leave things alone."

"So, do you know how I can get in touch with her or not?" He was about to take his plate to the sink, but his uncle took it from him.

"Not really. I'm still friends with her father. We see each other at the senior center, but we don't talk about our kids. All I know is she has some kind of store in Custer."

"Okay, that works." Immediately, he pulled out his cell phone and Googled her, finding out that the store she owned was an artist tourist shop. Interesting. "Found her." He stood. "I'll be back in a while."

"Jaden," Uncle Frank called from the sink, where he washed their dishes.

Already heading to the closet for a jacket, he turned back. "Yeah?"

"You're here for a few weeks, right?"

"Yep."

"Don't do anything stupid. She's a nice girl. Her parents are friends."

Jaden held his arms out. "I'm just going to talk to her. I owe her an apology, at least." What he didn't admit was that the brief encounter with her last night had left him unsettled, and he couldn't shake her from his mind.

Before heading out to see her, he stopped at Scheels and bought a couple of pairs of jeans, a few long-sleeved shirts, a knitted sweater, socks, underwear, a jacket, and shoes. He'd been wearing the same dirty suit for three days now.

He changed in his car. Then, he took the picturesque drive to Custer. The roads had been plowed early that morning, but fresh snow clung to the branches of the trees. The sun rising strongly in the late morning made some of the snow look like crystals. He's forgotten how pretty it was out here.

When he got to Keri's store, he parked and admired the cute little place with the sign that read Treasures of the Heart. Hmm. He entered the store, jingle bells marking his entrance, and saw her immediately, her head bent and her auburn hair cascading down as she worked on paperwork behind the counter. He'd forgotten how naturally beautiful she was, and something warm filled his chest.

She looked up with a smile that faded as soon as she noticed him. In fact, she looked angry.

"Nice place," he said.

"Turn around and go back out. We said all there was to say to each other last night."

Well, that was a pleasant greeting. "Mmm. Well, maybe you said all you wanted to say. I didn't say much, unfortunately. I was surprised to see you, and I kind of blew it." He picked up a piece of pottery—a red vintage truck, carrying a Christmas tree, and ran his index finger over the top. Cute.

"Blowing it is what you're good at."

He put the truck back on the shelf. "Keri," he said, stepping closer into the welcoming store filled with creative displays of enchanting artistic pieces, mostly Christmas-themed, and stopped in front of its unwelcoming owner. "Look, when I left, I was young and scared and stupid, and I needed to get out of here and figure out what I wanted and who I was. I didn't want to get trapped here—."

"With me."

"It had nothing to do with you. I just knew there was more out there. I didn't have anything to offer you."

Keri swallowed and looked down. "A man doesn't do what you did. You don't leave someone you supposedly love without saying a word. We'd been together for years."

"Exactly." He placed his hands on the counter and leaned closer to her. "All of high school. And I wasn't a man. How do two kids know what they want when all they've ever known was each other?"

"I knew." She shook her head. "I thought I knew. You made me realize I didn't know you at all. So, thank you. I would have made a huge mistake."

He wanted to say you're welcome, but that wouldn't have gone over well. He'd done her a favor even if she didn't see it. "I don't expect you to forgive me."

"I don't. But honestly, I stopped caring a long time ago." She closed the file she was working on and stepped around the counter.

"Good. Then, as two adults, we can put the past behind us and just be friends. I'd like that."

She stopped right in front of him. "You'd like that? Friends?" She laughed. "How long are you going to be here?"

"A couple of weeks, maybe three."

"You know those girls at the Christmas tree lot last night? They are my friends. We have years of history, years of being there for each other. We share good and bad times together. I cook for them and watch their kids when they have to work. Their husbands fix things that go wrong in my apartment. They are my friends. A guy I barely know who will be in town for two weeks can never be my friend."

Jaden wanted to joke that she obviously needed to see the value of a two-week friendship. It didn't include babysitting or fixing things. "How about I take you out to dinner as a peace offering? Call it what you will."

"Jaden, let me be perfectly clear. I don't want to have anything to do with you. If I don't see you again while you're in town for the next two weeks, that would be ideal. Okay?"

Not okay. He wanted to see her again. She was angry, obviously. But he hated it when women were upset with him. Though he may have commitment issues, he attempted to conclude each relationship positively, leaving women with the impression that their time together had been meaningful and that he had contributed something to their lives. He hadn't done that with Keri because he'd been young and foolish. He wanted to make it up to her. If she'd let him. "Okay, if that's what you want," he said. "But I have to tell you that you make it hard for a guy to apologize."

She gasped. "I haven't heard an apology." She put her hand up as if to block his words. "But I don't need one. I just want you to go."

"I'm *sorry*," he emphasized the word. "I apologize."

She shook her head as if disappointed.

Realizing that this was not going well, he took a step back. He admired her store, searching for pieces of who she'd become, but the eclectic art in this adorable store didn't give him any clues. He picked up a horseshoe wine rack that had a lot of character. It was unique, and though his uncle wasn't a big wine drinker, he would like it. "I'll take this."

"No, you won't. I'm not selling it to you."

"I need to buy my uncle a Christmas gift. He'd love this. Come on."

She studied him. "Jaden, you broke my heart. How can you stand there and act like what you did was nothing? Like we were nothing?"

"I know what I did. And I'm really, really sorry. I never wanted to hurt you."

He saw her face soften. "Finally, you sound like you mean it."

"If I could go back in time and do it again, I'd have been more open about what was going on inside me, how frightened I was about the future, how I didn't know what I wanted. I wouldn't have been such a coward. I still would have left; I have to be honest. I needed to go, but I should have talked to you."

Nodding, she took the wine rack and went behind the counter to ring it up. He handed her his credit card. Watching her, he tightened his lips in regret. She was part of his past, part of coming home, and it was a shame he'd hurt her, ruining the teenage memories they'd shared together and what they'd once had.

She wrapped the gift and placed it in a bag, handing it to him without meeting his eyes.

"Thanks, Keri. You really do have a nice place. I'm happy for you."

"Have a good visit with your uncle." She raised her gaze. "And leave me alone. I mean it."

CHAPTER FOUR

After work, Keri met her friends for drinks in downtown Rapid City at Murphy's Pub and Grill, a popular downtown hangout with a trendy vibe. The ladies were already enjoying their second beers when she got there. She pulled up a seat beside Sam.

"Brett stuck the popcorn so far up his nose it would have been easier for him to inhale it than to get it back out." Amanda finished her tale.

Everyone laughed and turned their attention to Keri.

"Finally, the woman who does not have to deal with snot and vomit joins us. "What's it like to spend your day with adults?" Amanda asked.

Keri signaled the server to bring her a beer and exhaled heavily as she settled into her chair.

"Long day?" Sam asked.

"Busy. I know people like to give unique gifts for Christmas, and I'm glad they choose art as the perfect gift. The problem is that they don't trust their taste. So, I find myself being a part journalist as I interview them about their loved ones. Oh, and the day started with Jaden stopping by."

"No way!" Sam said, followed by similar echoes. "Why?"

"To say he was sorry."

"A little too late,"

Keri shrugged. "I don't need his apologies after all this time, but I'll take them." He seemed sincere once he got around to really apologizing.

The server brought Keri her favorite Angry Orchard draft beer. Keri thanked her and asked for a bowl of chili and sweet potato fries.

"Did you notice all the scratches and bruises on him? I wonder what he's doing these days." Jenn said.

"Who knows? I don't care. He bought his uncle one of my horseshoe wine racks. And get this: He said he wanted to be friends." They all burst into a chorus of laughter. "Exactly my reaction. Isn't that the biggest cliché? Are all men that clueless, or just him?"

"All of them," Sam confirmed. "Patrick couldn't figure out why I was upset that he came back from being gone for four days at the base and wanted to leave again to go shooting with his friends. I asked him, 'Didn't you get enough shooting done while you were working?' and he stared at me with a stupid look on his face and said that's not his job."

"Did he go?" The high volume of Sheryl Crow's "If It Makes You Happy" made it difficult to have a conversation without raising her voice.

"Yes! So, tonight, I left him with the kids while he complained about not being able to sleep before he had to head back to the base."

"My husband wants nightly massages and sex," Jenn said, "and then he rolls over and goes to sleep and can't figure out why I'm not thrilled."

Keri smiled. "You all are making me kind of glad I'm not married." Her chili and fries arrived, and she dug in.

"Yes, be grateful," Sam said. "Hopefully, Jaden stays out of your way."

"He'll be gone in two or three weeks, and I'm sure it will be another ten years or so before I see him again." Which made her a little sad, not because she'd miss him, but because it never should have come to this. They were so close once. But that was a lifetime ago.

"Maybe you should have agreed to be 'his friend' so you could dump his ass this time," Sam said, picking up her glass and finishing her second beer.

"Hey, that's not a bad idea," Amanda said.

Keri laughed. "It's a terrible idea. Jaden and I will never be friends."

"Wait a minute, wait a minute," Sam said, putting her hand on Keri's arm. "That would teach him a lesson. If he contacts you again, go along with it, see how far he's willing to take this 'friendship,' and make him regret he lost you. Make him want you back, then invite him to the New Year's Eve party and publicly dump him in front of everyone."

"Right," Keri said, sipping her beer. Like she needed to play these games with a guy who wasn't even worth thinking about, much less spending enough time with him to entice him into a fake relationship.

They all nodded and made sounds of encouragement. "Oh, that would be justice. You've got to do it, Keri," Amanda said.

"I am not doing that."

Samantha leaned back in her seat and crossed her arms. "You were supposed to get married! He left you without a word of explanation. You cried in my arms for months, remember? And you still do not trust men."

"I trust men. I just haven't found one I want to marry. Besides, what is this, high school all over again?"

"If he's as shallow as he used to be, he won't really care, anyway. Do it."

Keri smiled. He really did deserve to be humiliated like she'd been. "He's not worth it. Let's change the subject, shall we? Did you all get your trees up?"

Jenn nodded. "She's right. Sounds kind of childish anyway, and Keri is too nice."

Everyone shared their cute stories of decorating their trees with their kids.

Jenn's last words bothered Keri. She *was* too nice, and it led to people taking advantage of her. Something else that bothered her, though maybe bothered wasn't the right word, saddened was more honest, and it was that she had spent the morning before work playing Christmas music, sipping coffee, and filling her small apartment with Christmas spirit. Alone. She enjoyed it, but she would have enjoyed it so much more with kids.

Over the past couple of years, her perspective on kids has changed. She went from finding them cute to wanting some of her own. Lately, however, a deep emptiness has settled in her heart and even in the pit of her stomach. It was as if an invisible child was there, a ghost of the baby she should have had. The thought that she'd missed the opportunity to bring a soul into the world left her with an odd sense of unease, as if she had failed her own child.

This had started about nine months ago when she turned twenty-nine. She realized it was her last year in her twenties, and she still didn't have a child. What they say about ticking clocks is real. She'd never imagined it would feel so awful.

"Hey, you okay?" Sam said, placing a hand over hers.

"Sure."

"He was bound to come back someday."

"I know. It's okay. He doesn't bother me."

Sam studied her, then leaned the side of her head against Keri's. "You're lying just a little."

"Maybe just a little." Keri smiled and watched her friends. They were funny and a little crazy, and she loved them. She didn't need a husband and kids when she had so many people who loved her. She placed an arm around Sam and focused on what she had.

CHAPTER FIVE

J aden spent the following morning sitting around his uncle's house, making a few calls to clients who were interested in purchasing his Bugatti La Voiture Noire, which he'd bought when it was first released in 2019. This hypersports car reminded him of a Batmobile. It was a black beauty with a powerful quad-turbo 8-litre W16 engine. Collectors loved not only the look but the 1479 horsepower and 1600 newton-metres of torque. He hoped to sell it before Christmas. A rock star's wife was hot for this car, and her husband "deserved" it, according to her. Who was he to argue? Give the man what he deserves. But she still hadn't committed. If he was lucky, he'd be able to put a big bow on the car and have it delivered to her before the twenty-fifth.

He'd also been on the phone for about an hour with his insurance agent. As he predicted, his agent had a fit and told him his rates were going to skyrocket.

But by mid-morning, he was bored. He wasn't used to sitting around, wasting time. Working and traveling as much as he did meant that he didn't have many friends to hang out with. He had business associates, yes, and plenty of events to attend. And, of course, beautiful women to enjoy, but he never slowed down enough to realize that he didn't actually have friends, especially in this town, not after staying away for ten years.

He couldn't even go for a run. Not with all the snow on the ground. Well, he could go for a walk or a hike with the right shoes.

"Hey, Uncle Frank, I'm going to go out and get better shoes. You want me to pick up anything for you?"

"I'm okay. I should go to the senior center, but I'm tired, so I'll probably just watch TV and take a nap."

"You mean, what you've been doing all morning? Come on, get dressed. I'll drop you off at the senior center."

"Not today."

"You're letting yourself get old. Come on, get up, get those muscles working."

Frank chuckled. "You go exercise your muscles. Mine are happily resting. Besides, a friend of mine is going to stop by later."

Jaden knew his uncle kept himself busy. He didn't look bad for a guy in his late sixties, but it didn't take long for a man to start to feel old and give up on life. Uncle Frank had a lot of good years ahead of him.

Jaden patted his uncle on the shoulder. "Okay, Uncle Frank."

Jaden went back to Scheels and found a pair of warm hiking boots, then decided to look for a handsaw. When he cut the trunk of the Christmas tree to fit it in the tree stand, he noticed that his uncle's saw was getting kind of old. But as he searched the Home and Yard aisle, he didn't find a real handsaw, only folding pruning saws that weren't very strong. He'd have to go to Lowes, maybe.

As he turned to leave, he noticed a guy who looked a lot like Keri's dad. When the man glanced at him, probably wondering why some fool was staring, Jaden realized it was definitely Keri's dad.

Jaden waved. "Hi, Mr. Anderson."

"Jaden? Well, look at you. Frank didn't tell me you were back in town."

Jaden stepped closer and was about to put his hand out to shake, but that seemed awkward. Mr. Anderson held a small sliding saw in his hand anyway. "Yes, sir. I came to spend Christmas with him. How are you?"

"Not bad. Enjoying retirement. Keeping busy."

Jaden smiled. "Good, good." He didn't know what else to say. They stood staring at each other. Soft Christmas music played in the store.

"Keri know you're back?"

Why did he know the question would come? "I ran into her, yes. But she wasn't too happy to see me."

"I imagine not. Things didn't end well between you two."

"They didn't end at all. That's the problem. My fault."

Mr. Anderson raised an eyebrow and gave him a pointed look. "You broke my girl's heart."

Jaden glanced at the saw in the older man's hands. It was never good to run into a woman's father after a relationship was over, but it was especially bad when he had a weapon in his hands. "I know. I told her I was sorry. She was still angry."

"You know, Jaden, we all loved you in our family. You were a good boy. I don't think she's angry anymore, and she's probably not hurt either, but she was when you left."

"I know." He was starting to realize what an asshole he'd been.

"No, you don't. She was crushed and cried for months. You were engaged, and then you disappeared. She waited and waited for you to come back. Do you know that?"

He did now. And damn it, he felt like shit. "Mr. Anderson, I was a young boy. What did I know about being engaged? I just gave her a ring because, you know, guys do that. Be my girl kind of thing. I . . . shit, I don't know if I ever intended to get married. I know that sounds horrible."

Mr. Anderson shook his head. "You really are your uncle's kid. Except stupider. And Frank is my friend, so I can say that. But that man never understood women. Apparently, you don't either."

Couldn't argue with him there. "I don't know what to say, sir."

Mr. Anderson shrugged. "Nothing you can say after so many years."

"I'm going to go pay for my shoes. It was . . . nice to see you."

"Hold up. I'm going to checkout, too. I make these wooden statues for Keri's store. Little animals and things tourists like. She has an art shop up in Custer."

They headed to the checkout stands. "I know. I was there."

He angled his head and glanced at him but didn't say what he was thinking.

They each paid for their items and walked outside together to their cars.

"Well." Jaden held out his hand this time. "I wish you well."

Mr. Anderson nodded and shook Jaden's hand. Then he got into his car, drove a few feet, and his car made a horrible sound and stopped. Opening his driver-side door, he said, "My car died."

"Dead battery, maybe?" Jaden said, though, it didn't sound like a battery issue.

He sighed. "Who knows? I don't think it's the battery."

"May I?" Jaden pointed to the hood. He looked inside and groaned. "Mr. Anderson, try to turn it on again." When he did, the camshaft didn't turn at all, even though the crankshaft was spinning. He waved at him to stop cranking the engine. "I think your timing belt snapped. Has it been making any strange sounds?"

"A few clicking sounds, yeah."

Jaden nodded. "You'll have to have a mechanic look at it, but I'm sure if you take the timing belt cover off, you'll see that it's gone."

"Hell," Mr. Anderson said. He pulled out his cell phone. "I'll call the tow truck and take it to the repair shop."

Jaden felt bad for him. When a timing belt breaks, it's bad news for the engine. The pistons, valves, and cylinder heads are probably damaged, which means major instantaneous damage to the engine. Jaden stayed with him while he waited for the tow.

Once the car was hooked to the tow truck, Jaden asked, "Do you want a ride home?"

"Ah, sure, that would be nice. My mechanic said he can't even look at the car until tomorrow." He'd been on the phone with the repair shop while waiting for the tow truck to arrive.

"I'm sorry, Mr. Anderson."

As they drove, Mr. Anderson filled him in on some of the changes in town and shared that he and Uncle Frank were part of a ping-pong team at the senior center. "I'm way better than him. He has no coordination," he said.

Jaden hid a smile.

When Jaden pulled into his driveway, Mr. Anderson asked, "Do you want to come inside?"

Jaden shook his head. "No, I'm going to go on a little hike. But thank you. And good luck with the repair. I fear you'll need a new engine."

"Well, if that's true, it might not be worth fixing it." He shook his head. "That's all I need, I car payment."

"Hopefully, I'm wrong," Jaden said.

"I hope so. Well, feel free to stop by anytime, and thanks for staying with me and for the ride."

He wouldn't be stopping by again, but Jaden thanked him and moved on.

Jaden parked in Founder's Park which had multiple dirt trails, creeks, and a nice hill to climb. He spent about an hour making his way to the top of M Hill, named for the big white M that greeted him. From the top, he could see the entire city. He sat on a rock wall and admired his hometown. He and Keri used to climb up here together on weekends and have picnics – well, a bag of chips and a Coke.

The town had grown in the last ten years. Had he missed it? Not really. If he was honest, he hadn't missed anything or anyone. Growing a business, struggling to get capital and find investors, and building a clientele had taken so much effort. He didn't have time to miss anything. Obviously, he'd thought of his uncle and called for advice or just to talk because he loved him. He'd been more of a father than an uncle, but Frank had encouraged Jaden to find himself and to live his life. "You don't owe me anything, Boy," he'd said. "Go do what you need to do, and don't worry about me." Jaden had taken the order literally and now wondered if that had been a mistake.

He thought about how he should have missed Keri. And maybe he had, especially at first. But after high school, she'd enrolled at Black Hills State University while he decided not to go to college. His uncle didn't have the money, and Jaden couldn't see the point in getting loans to learn more of what he'd already learned in high school.

He got a job selling used and upscale cars to businessmen, medical professionals, and people who had money. After about a year, his boss, impressed with Jaden's sales abilities, offered him a position as a manager at his larger Denver showroom, where he sold new and luxury cars. He would triple his salary and teach him the business.

Keri seemed so busy with her new life and college friends that he'd started to feel like he was losing her. That was part of the reason he'd proposed six months before he left. It had been an immature way to hold on to her, and she'd been so excited and happy, immediately saying yes and planning the event that had no date.

When he was offered the opportunity to make more money, to do something better with his life, he hadn't even remembered that he'd asked Keri to marry him. He spoke with his uncle, and two weeks later, he'd packed his stuff and left.

When he got settled in Denver in a little single apartment, he thought of calling Keri, but he decided it was best to let things die. They were going their separate ways, and it was for the best.

The first woman he'd slept with after he'd left had been a woman who worked for his boss. She was about ten years older than him. Jaden had acted sure of himself, arrogant, and had come on so strong that he wondered why she hadn't laughed in his face. But instead, she'd invited him to her house. They'd had pretty bad sex, and after, he could only think of Keri. He thought sex with other women would make him forget her, but he'd been wrong. Those first few years, he'd slept with so many women, almost defiantly. He was young and free, so why not? But he always felt empty. Eventually, he stopped thinking of Keri, but he never found a woman who really, sincerely, interested him.

Sometimes, it was hard not to wish you could go back in time to do things again the right way. Maybe he could make it up to Keri now, if she gave him the chance. He'd been unfair, unkind, selfish, cowardly. He sighed as he stared out at the quiet city, knowing that berating himself now wasn't going to fix anything.

Listening to birds sing, and the breeze blowing through the leaves, he felt a sense of peace. He didn't have to be anyone he wasn't here. No worries about appearance or money or power. No one cared about that here, not like in Los Angeles.

After sitting too long and getting cold, he walked down without running into another person. Only he was crazy enough to be outside today. His nose ran, and his fingers were numb.

When he got to his rented car, he cranked up the heater and thawed out his fingers. He blew his nose, took off his beanie, and fluffed out his short hair.

Now what? Shit, no wonder he didn't take vacations. All he wanted was to get warm. Yep, a warm blanket, the TV, and the couch. Sounded good to him.

Keri took her Labradoodle for a walk along the creek that ran at the bottom of Founder's Park, on Omaha Blvd. For a second, she thought she saw Jaden approaching the trail, but she figured she was seeing him everywhere now. She had to get that man out of her mind.

"Come on, Mochi," she called her Golden Doodle, and they continued walking along the creek. She had a doctor's appointment with her OBGYN today, so her only employee was opening the store for her. She'd thought hard about her decision to have a child by herself.

A child needed a mother and a father, but if she never got married, if she never found the right guy, did she want to die childless? She'd decided that no, she didn't. She would love her future baby enough for two people. Her brother could be a male role model and so could her friend's husbands. She didn't need a husband.

So, today was her second appointment with a doctor to discuss the possibility of getting pregnant on her own, with donor contribution, of course. She'd received a catalog from a sperm bank, looked into the cost, and she'd chosen a possible donor for intrauterine insemination. It all sounded so cold and medical, and she supposed it was.

The process of shopping for characteristics from an anonymous donor also felt a bit odd. They listed things like his GPA, physical features, race, interests, and general health to help women decide on attributes that would be half of their child's biology.

She'd chosen donor 1578, who was a medical student, artistic, had a big family, and liked animals. How would that affect her future kid? She wasn't sure. He also had a fairly clean medical history. Aside from diabetes that ran in his family, no one had died of a heart attack or had other diseases. That was good.

Today, after one more physical exam, she'd be ready to order the specimens and begin the process. She was excited and nervous. All of this, she'd done without sharing her secret with anyone, not even Samantha, who knew everything about her. Not even her mother, who might have a fit if she found out. She'd tell everyone if the procedure was successful and she became pregnant.

Why share anything until then? If it happened as she hoped, it would be too late for anyone to talk her out of it.

Keri dropped her dog off at home and then headed to the doctor's office. They drew blood, checked her blood pressure, and went through the regular check-up routine.

The gynecologist sat in front of her and smiled. She was a cute, thin lady with short black hair and big black eyes. "At almost thirty, you'll want to know a few things. Or at least, I feel I should share a few points with you. First, there's no reason to suspect that you have any fertility issues, but I do want to remind you that as we get older, fertility naturally declines."

Keri nodded. Sitting on the exam table with her legs dangling down, she felt both like a little girl and an old woman who had to be told her eggs were going to dry up soon.

"Also, you could be at higher risk for miscarriage or birth defects."

"I'm not even thirty yet?"

"It's not likely. But I want to give you all the warnings," Doctor Pruitt said. "Artificial insemination is costly, and there's no guarantee that it will take, and I'm giving you some possible scenarios for you to consider before you commit."

"Okay."

"If you don't get pregnant right away and you continue to try during the next few years, you should be aware of the statistics. After age 35, the chances of having a baby with Down's Syndrome is 1 in 100, and when you compare it to women under 25 where it's 1 in 1250, you can see that the odds increase dramatically."

Keri nodded. "Then I don't want to keep waiting. You're not dissuading me; you're making me see how urgent it is for me to do it now."

"I'm not trying to dissuade you, Keri. I only want you to understand that this is a medical procedure, and it might or might not be successful immediately. We might have to inseminate you multiple times. If you get pregnant, you could still suffer a miscarriage, and if you give birth, there could be complications. Understand?"

"I understand. I want to at least try."

Doctor Pruitt nodded and made a note in her chart. "Okay, then. You'll order the specimens, and we'll get started. Let's begin after Christmas. How does that sound?"

"Can we begin right away? Next week? I'll be ovulating. I've been tracking it."

"If you're sure. Make an appointment, and I'll see you next week."

Keri left the clinic, excited and nervous, hoping she wasn't making a huge mistake. But how could bringing life into this world be a mistake? How could wanting a baby to love be wrong?

CHAPTER SIX

A fter napping and watching TV all day, Jaden needed to do something else. He decided to find Keri, invite her to dinner, and start making up for being such a jerk. But he still didn't know where she lived, so he drove back to her father's house.

Keri's mother answered the door, and like her husband, she seemed surprised to see him, but surely Mr. Anderson had told her that Jaden had returned to town and had given him a ride home that morning.

"I wonder if I can speak to your husband."

"Sure, come in. Jaden." She closed the door and invited him into the kitchen. "Look at you, all grown up."

Jaden chuckled. "Yes, ma'am."

"It's been so long. Where do you live now? What have you been doing with your life?"

"I have a business in California, and I—."

"Who was at the door?" Mr. Anderson entered the kitchen, his brow furrowed. "Jaden? What's wrong? We were just going to go to bed."

"Oh, I'm sorry. I didn't realize it was so late." It was 8 pm.

A big golden poodle-like dog came and nudged his hand with its nose. Jaden petted the dog's head and scratched behind his ears.

"That's okay," Mrs. Anderson said. "Sit down. We're waiting for Keri to pick up Mochi, so we're not exactly going to sleep immediately."

He pulled up a kitchen chair and sat, continuing to rub the dog down with both his hands. When he stopped, Mochi placed his head on Jaden's lap. Keri was coming to pick the dog up? Perfect. "I wondered if the repair shop told you what was wrong with the car."

"You came out here tonight to get an update on my car?"

Sounded stupid, but he needed a reason to be here. And suddenly, he got an idea. "It's just that my job is to buy and sell cars. Super expensive luxury cars, but sometimes, people also give me other cars in trade."

"You want to sell me a car?" Mr. Anderson asked, seeming a bit perturbed.

"Ah no, Sir. I have an older car in my warehouse, one that I own because a client didn't want it. He insisted I take it as a partial payment on a car that he did want. It's been sitting in my warehouse for over a year. I don't drive it. I can't sell it because I don't sell used cars. If your car can't be fixed or if it's going to be too expensive to fix and it won't be worth it, I can give you this car."

Both Mr. and Mrs. Anderson looked at each other, and Mr. Anderson cleared his throat. "Do you know how odd this sounds?"

"Yes, but it's not. You'd be doing me a favor. I don't know what to do with this vehicle. It's taking up space I need for other cars. I have to pay yearly registration fees. And it depreciates in value the longer I hold on to it."

"But why give it to *me*, Jaden?"

Because I didn't know what the hell to say to get your daughter's phone number. But the more he thought about it, the more sense it made. He *wanted* to help Mr. Anderson, and the man needed the car, the one thing Jaden had. "You both were so kind to me when I was a kid. How many meals did you serve me?" He pointed at Mrs. Anderson. "I mean, why not? I know cars, and to be honest, your engine will be beyond repair." Jaden straightened in his chair. "I'm not bragging, but I'm a pretty wealthy man. If I can't help old friends, then what's the point of having all this money? Please, accept this gift."

The front door opened, and the dog ran to jump on Keri as she appeared in the entry. She laughed and told him to get down. "I hope he was a good boy," she said. Her smile died on her lips when she noticed Jaden at the kitchen table. "What are you doing here?"

"My car broke down at the mall, and he gave me a ride home," Mr. Anderson said. "And now he's come back to offer me a used car."

Keri's mouth opened, and he wasn't sure if she was going to say something or was just shocked. Then she shook her head. "My father does not need your car."

Jaden offered her a smile. "I think he does."

"Get out," she said, pointing at the door.

Her pink cheeks darkened on her pretty face. Jaden wasn't sure what to say. He wanted to apologize and take her out to dinner, but all he seemed to do was make her angrier.

"Keri," her mother interrupted. "Calm down."

"I can't believe you're in my parent's house. What part of stay away from me did you not understand?"

"I'm trying to help."

"We don't need your help. Tell him, Daddy."

Mr. Anderson looked uncomfortable, but he nodded. "I appreciate the offer, Jaden, but Keri's right. I'll fix my car and keep it. Thank you just the same."

Jaden stood and nodded. "If you change your mind, let me know. It's no bother. I can have my employee drive it here. He could be here in a couple of days."

"You have a hard time understanding the word, no, don't you?" Keri asked.

"Can we step outside for just a second?" he asked her.

"For what?"

"Because I'm enjoying talking to you so much that I want to keep doing it."

The older couple said goodbye as he headed to the door. Keri didn't move, so he raised an eyebrow. "You want me to leave, right? So, come out here with me for a second."

Keri really wanted to slap him. He was unbelievable. Mochi was going nuts because he wanted out. Her parents, her poor parents, stared at the two of them, not knowing what to say. And he stood at the door, comfortable, entitled, arrogantly waiting for her to follow him out.

"I'll be back in a second," she said to her parents, and as soon as she stepped out onto the porch, she started telling him what a low-life, manipulative, condescending asshole he was.

But he started laughing. Laughing. As if she'd just told him the best joke of his life.

"What the hell is so funny?"

"Oh honey, you are. Listen, let me buy you dinner."

She wondered for a minute if this man suffered from mental illness. Did he lack the ability to comprehend? But she realized that he just didn't care that she didn't want him around. He didn't care that she couldn't stand him. He only cared about what he wanted because he couldn't put himself into anyone's shoes but his own.

Suddenly, the conversation with her friends and their idea to lead him on and make him think she was interested, only to dump his ass, sounded so perfect, the humiliation so deserved, that she couldn't resist. "You want to buy me dinner tonight?"

"I do."

"Restaurants close early in town. Did you forget?"

"A drink, maybe?"

She crossed her arms and glared at him. "Dinner. Tomorrow."

He seemed surprised but happy. A huge grin cracked his stupid face. "Tomorrow! You got it. Can I say one more thing?"

She shrugged. "I'm freezing, but yes, let's keep talking." The distant sounds of traffic and the gentle breeze that blew snow off the pine trees were faint, making their voices seem even louder. Or maybe it was her angry voice she was sure everyone in the neighborhood could hear.

"I know how you feel about me. You have every right to be angry, to hate me, to want me to stay away from you, but don't make your dad pay for my mistakes. If the cost to fix his car is going to be too much, and I anticipate that it will be, let me give him my car."

"He doesn't need charity."

"Keri," he said, scratching the back of his head and pleading, "It's not charity. It's a gift. It's a car that someone gave me, and I don't use it. I don't want it. It's taking up space in my warehouse. It only has about fifty thousand miles on it, but it's not worth selling, at least for me. It would be perfect for your dad. Just think about it. You can keep hating me, okay? But let him have the car."

He sounded so damned sincere. "Jaden, we don't want anything from you."

He sighed. "Fine. I don't get it, but fine. Where do I pick you up for dinner tomorrow?"

She pointed behind her parents' house. "The apartments three blocks down. I'm in 317."

"Okay, 6 p.m. work for you?"

"I can't wait," she said, full of sarcasm, but he smiled and winked before stepping down the stairs and walking to his car. Her parents' Christmas lights rotated from red to yellow to green, making him change colors as he got further away.

CHAPTER SEVEN

K eri dressed in simple jeans and a warm red and gold sweater in honor of the Christmas season, then yanked the sweater off and slipped on a burgundy ruched V-neck blouse that dipped low and screamed, "Look at my breasts."

"Ugh, why am I doing this?" she asked herself as she stared into the mirror. Part of her wanted to look amazing so that he could see what he had given up. And the other part thought it was stupid and childish because it didn't matter what he thought.

She wasn't even sure why she agreed to do this. Probably because he made her so angry, he was so arrogant, so intrusive, and so clueless that she wanted to do to him what he'd done to her. Make him want her. Make him love her. Then, leave him to deal with the pain.

She applied a little makeup and fluffed her hair, knowing that no matter what she did, she couldn't make him feel something he didn't and never would.

With a sigh, she grabbed her purse and jacket and headed to the living room to wait for him to arrive.

And he did, right on time.

"Let's go," she said, as he was about to enter her apartment. She kissed Mochi on the nose and told him to lie down on his bed. Mochi moaned but turned around and curled up on his warm, fluffy cushion.

"There's no hurry," he said.

"Are we going to go eat or not? I'm hungry."

"Right." He nodded, placed a hand on her back, then took it off and scratched the back of his head. "Lead the way."

She climbed down the stairs with him following behind. He smelled good. He'd never worn cologne when he was younger. And he looked amazing in dark slacks, a dress shirt with a tie, and a sweater over it.

"The snow is melting, but it's still chilly," he said, zipping his jacket when they got to his car.

"Where do you live? Are you not used to the cold anymore?"

When they got to his car, he opened the door, and she got inside.

He turned the vehicle on. "I live mostly in California, but I travel a lot. I was in the Denver area out by Elisabeth earlier this week visiting a friend." He pulled out into the street. "It's where I got in an accident."

She gazed at him and the cuts and bruises that were healing on his face. "You were in an accident?"

"Yep. Totaled my rental car. Lucky, I didn't die, they tell me. I think they thought I had. But I walked away with some bruised ribs and my handsome face a bit messed up." He smiled.

"Hmm."

"Where to? Feel like a nice steak?"

"Sure."

"Is Dakota Steakhouse still in business? I could never afford to go there as a kid or to take you anywhere nice. We could go there."

"It's still there."

He reached across and patted her knee. "Let's go there then."

She moved her leg away. "Wherever."

He got on the I-90 and headed out toward the restaurant. They drove in silence, and she looked out of the window. Being in a car with him felt unreal. "So, did you really almost die?"

He shrugged. "All I remember is driving way too fast, seeing something cross in front of me—turns out it was a deer. I hit it. The back end of the car lifted, and I started rolling. Next thing I know, I'm in the hospital with a bit of concussion, my side killing me, and feeling really weird."

"Wow. Is that why you decided to come home?"

"You mean, did the near-death experience make me want to touch base with my uncle?" With a lopsided grin, he shrugged again. "I don't really know. I just had this urge to come back." He pulled off the ramp and parked in the restaurant parking lot. Then he turned the car off and gazed at her. "To tell you the truth, some years I don't remember to call him. And other years, I call every month or so. Just depends on when I remember and how busy I am."

She shook her head, wondering what she ever saw in him. "You must be so proud of yourself for being such an independent man of the world who doesn't need anyone."

He reached across and eased some hair away from her forehead. "I didn't say I didn't need anyone?"

She refused to flinch or turn away and instead stared him down. "Right. You just have a bad memory. You should make a note for yourself and set a reminder on your phone: call my uncle. He gave up his whole life for you, or did you forget that too?"

He eased back. "I'll never forget that." Their gazes remained locked for a moment, then he offered a small smile. "But good idea. I might just set a reminder to come visit him every other month. I'm starting to like being back here."

Great. "Let's go in."

Jaden opened the door to the restaurant and placed a hand on her back, guiding her inside first. He didn't miss that she hurried past him and away from his touch. He wasn't trying to make her uncomfortable. Somehow, he wanted to break the ice. Women always told him he was a nice guy, and he really tried to be. He might have issues with commitment, but he honestly wanted women to be happy and enjoy being with him when they were together. More so, this was true with Keri.

The hostess led them to a table tucked away in a cozy corner, ensuring that they could enjoy their conversation in complete privacy. The restaurant had elaborate Christmas decorations, creating a festive and welcoming atmosphere. "Man, this is cool. It's dumb, but I'm excited to be here. I could barely afford to buy you a Big Mac when we were in high school."

"Jaden, I never cared what you bought me. Or if you had money."

Nice of her to say. "I cared."

"You were in high school, and when we got out, you got an entry-level job with that car guy. Of course, you didn't have a lot of money."

"Well, tonight, let's live it up. Order anything. Order everything!"

She smiled. The first authentic smile he'd gotten from her. "I'll start with a glass of wine."

"Perfect."

They ordered their drinks, and when she took her jacket off, he took in that hot shirt she wore. He tried not to look for too long. "So, tell me about your store."

"It's an art consignment store. Local artists bring me their things, and if they are appropriate for the store, I sell them. It's a lot of fun. I meet great people who are always happy, vacationing, and appreciate art."

"Are you open year-round?"

"Sort of. Definitely during the summer. I usually close down in January and February."

He nodded. They ordered their food, and then he looked around. What was there to say to a woman he barely knew? Their only connection was the past. "How did your tree look?"

"Oh, my Christmas tree . . . I put it up the night I got it. It's just me, so I don't do much decorating at home. I save that for the store."

"Why is it just you?"

Her eyes met his, then skidded away. She took a sip of wine. "Not an appropriate question."

"Why not? I'm alone because I suck at relationships. What's your deal?"

"I must suck at them, too."

"I find that hard to imagine."

"Really? Because I've been so nice to you?"

He covered one of her hands. "You have the right to be angry, upset, and to give me hell."

She eased her hand back. "I just haven't met the right person. I date sometimes, but I don't want to settle, you know what I mean? One guy I liked drank a little too much, and I thought that it wasn't so bad, but should I marry a guy who is not so bad? And it's been the same with others."

"It's good to know what you want," he said, angling his head. "You shouldn't settle."

"Yeah, but I'm getting older. At some point, I think everyone settles if they don't want to be alone." She laughed. "Why am I talking about this with you? Never mind."

"Sometimes it's better to be alone."

"We agree on something," she said, holding out her wine glass to touch it to his.

Their food arrived, and they were both happy to dig in. He ordered a massive steak with a baked potato, beans, and a side of corn. It was delicious.

"So, you sell expensive cars?"

"Mm," he wiped his lips. "Yep. When I left here, it was because the guy I was working for offered me the opportunity to travel to Colorado to acquire cars for him to sell and manage his business. He thought I was good at negotiating and making deals. I worked for him for a while and eventually branched out on my own. I've met super wealthy people who enjoy having collections. So, I buy and hold luxury cars and sell them at a profit."

"Colorado. So that's where you went?"

Jaden nodded, not wanting to talk about him leaving again. "I also like sports cars. I buy race cars, and I've driven a few. Not professionally, just for fun."

She took a bite of her steak and then a drink of water. Wiping her lips with the napkin on her lap, she widened her eyes, "Didn't know you had such an interest in cars."

"I didn't either until I got into it. It's more the thrill of buying something others want and trying to find the right buyer. Kind of like you. Doesn't it make you happy when the right person buys a piece of art you like?"

Nodding, she gazed at him. "It does, actually."

"These cars are a gorgeous piece of art, I tell you. You've got to see them in person to appreciate the designs, the engineering, and the spectacular machines they are. I'm talking Rolls Royce, Bentley, Maserati, Ferrari, the crème de la crème."

Keri had ordered another glass of wine. She sat back with a lazy smile, swirling what was left in her glass. "Hmm, I'd like to see one."

"Okay, let's fly out to my warehouse. I'll show you the ones I have right now."

She laughed. "I didn't mean literally, just that I'd like to see a Rolls Royce, for example. I never have. And you're right, I do love art."

"Then let's go."

She put her glass down. "No."

"Okay." But he leaned in, eyeing her across the table. "But if we did, we could pick up that car I have for your dad. You sure?"

"I'm sure. This was delicious. And it wasn't complete torture being with you. Thank you for dinner." She smiled.

"I'm glad you enjoyed it."

"I did. But we should go. I need to take Mochi out for a little walk before bed."

Jaden stood and helped her with her jacket, glancing down the V of her shirt. She eased her hair back and caught him looking. She raised an eyebrow. "Are you checking me out?"

"No, ah, sort of. Sorry. You look good."

But she didn't get annoyed. She laughed. "That's okay. This shirt is ridiculous. I wore it to show you what you missed by dumping me." She wrapped her coat around her.

"Well," he said. "Nice job. I definitely couldn't resist a quick look." He opened the door to the restaurant so she could walk out. "And I didn't dump you. Technically, we're still engaged."

She really laughed this time. "Of course, we are."

When Keri opened the front door, Mochi whined and jumped on his hind legs. She hurried inside, pulled the leash off the hook in her entry, and grabbed a hat. Jaden insisted on staying until she walked the dog, so he followed beside her as Mochi excitedly bounced down the sidewalk, in and out of the snow that had been shoveled to the side.

Jaden laughed. "Man, he loves the snow."

"He loves walks and never seems to get cold. I'm not sure if all Labradoodles are the same, but he'd stay outside all day digging in the snow if we let him. When he gets inside, I have to wrap him in towels to dry his fur."

Jaden shoved his hands into his jacket pockets and looked up at the sky as they walked.

"You don't have to do this, you know," Keri said.

"I don't mind. After all the food we ate, I can use a little walk."

"I mean, try to be friendly and hang out with me. We're good. I won't say I forgive you, but we are in the past, and we can stay there."

"Can I share something really weird?"

"Okay.

"After my accident, I was knocked out, I guess. I don't really remember, but I have these visions, like I was remembering you. Other women too, but you were the one I wanted to see."

"You were dreaming about me?"

"Not really dreaming. It was . . . visions. I can't explain it. And then, as soon as I got here, I ran into you. Isn't that strange?"

"It's a small town." They turned the corner. She usually took the dog around the block, and that was far enough for him to relieve himself, especially when it was cold.

"I know. But what I'm getting at is that maybe I am supposed to hang out with you. Apologize. Make things right."

"You can't make things right. But you've apologized. If it's something you had to get off your chest, you've done it." They turned the corner and headed back toward her apartment.

"I guess." He smiled. "You don't think it's weird?"

They stopped at the entry to the apartment building while the dog sniffed around. "It's a little weird. But you said you were close to death. Maybe we have regrets when something like that happens. Maybe I'm really one of your regrets."

"Maybe you are," he said softly, gazing at her as if studying her face.

"Thanks. In a way, that does make me feel better." Imagine that. Could it be she wanted him to suffer a little like she had? "Good night, Jaden, and thanks for dinner."

"Night." He held up a hand and headed to his car.

As she was getting ready for bed, she opened her closet and reached for an old box from high school. It had yearbooks and pictures of her and her friends and of Jaden. She sat on her bed and opened it, pulling out the photos she'd never thrown out. The two of them at football games, on the bleachers. Jaden kissing her, tipping her back at a school dance. Jaden spending Christmases and summers at her house. Photos of them both with her family. She stared at the pictures and ran her fingers over the glossy finish. He'd been so sweet back then, and she so innocent. She'd loved him deeply, honestly, and completely. It was a pure love, unconditional, the way only first love could be. Sighing, she dropped the old photos back into the box where they'd been packed away for years. "Why didn't you stay gone?" she whispered.

CHAPTER EIGHT

Keri had the most customers on the weekend, but they were not early shoppers, which was great because this allowed her to spend the morning running errands or taking care of personal tasks before starting her work-day. So, she got up early Saturday morning to buy her dad a Christmas present and buy groceries before driving to her shop.

Her mom was easy to buy for. She'd already bought her exercise sneakers and a watch to count her steps, gift-cards at Ulta for make-up, a few books, a hard drive for her computer because she saved so many photos she needed more computer space, and a box of chocolate because you had to have chocolate on Christmas Day.

Her dad was tougher to buy for, but he wanted a recliner with a drink holder on the arm. Her mother said she'd throw him and his chair out if he bought one, but Keri knew her mom would accept it if it was tasteful and fit her style. At the furniture store, Keri found a brown leather chair that would blend in well with her mother's tan couch and rocking glider. She placed the order, and the furniture store promised to deliver it before Christmas.

When she left the furniture store, she popped into the grocery market to buy milk, eggs, and vegetables. She made herself a big salad as soon as she got home, and finally, she dropped Mochi at her parents' house on her way to work. Her mom would entertain Mochi, who loved playing catch, watching mom cook, and sleeping by the fireplace. Though sometimes Keri took him to the store with her, he seemed happier staying at her parents' house.

Keri made a brief stop at Sam's place on her way to work.

"Hey, I brought you the latest Lisa Jewell novel. I finished reading it."

"Ooh, thanks. I've got a Michael Connelly. Want it?"

"I'll take it. Before I go, I have to tell you I had dinner with Jaden last night."

Sam's eyes widened. "No way. I didn't think you were going to go through with the whole leading him on thing."

"I wasn't, but he annoyed me to the point that I agreed to go out with him. It was a one-time thing, and I think we can both move on now."

"Oh really? You've got closure, huh?"

"Not really. But first of all, he's not going to fall in love with me by New Year. And if he did, I wouldn't have the heart to hurt him. Plus, he's only staying until Christmas, I think."

"If you can stand to be around him, you should absolutely give him a taste of his own medicine." Sam put an arm around her. "As nice and sweet as you are, he'll be in love with you again before the end of the week." She pinched Keri's cheek. "How could he resist you?"

Keri laughed. "I can definitely reel him in if I want." She was joking, of course. Jaden couldn't be reeled in. Otherwise, he never would have left. But last night, in bed, she couldn't stop thinking about what he'd shared.

About dreaming of her after the accident, or having a vision, or whatever it was. Why her?

Maybe it was just a line, and he was playing her. In town for two weeks, he had nothing to do; if he could convince her to indulge in a brief romance with him, why wouldn't he? And she'd be the fool a second time. She definitely couldn't trust him.

Keri rested her chin on the back of her hands. "Getting even with a guy for not wanting me isn't exactly fair, is it?"

Sam sat at the table across from her. "The idiot moved on without a word. It wasn't that he didn't want you; it's that he left you planning a wedding, dreaming of the children you'd have together, and wondering what happened."

Keri lifted her head and nodded sadly. "Yeah."

"Every time I remember, it makes my blood boil. Don't let him sweet-talk you into forgiving him. If you don't want to get back at him, don't, but then stay away from him. He's poison."

Sam was right. After one dinner, Keri had almost decided he'd had a right to leave the way he had. "I'd better get to work."

"And Keri?"

"Hmm."

"He was a fool. Anyone who wouldn't want you deserves to have his head examined."

Keri chuckled. "Thanks, friend." She gave her a hug and headed to her car. Her cell phone rang as she got behind the wheel."

"Keri, it's mom. Your dad's car is definitely dead, and he doesn't know if he wants to spend the money to fix it. Can you pick him up at the repair shop and drop him off at the senior center before you go to work?"

Keri glanced at the time on her phone. She'd be a little late opening the store, but that was okay.

"Sure. Are you going to pick him up?"

"Yes, but he'll be there three or four hours. That way, I won't have to go out twice."

"No problem."

The night with Keri had gone marvelously well! Jaden wanted to see her again. But he also wanted to spend time with his uncle since he wasn't sure when he'd see him again. Jaden had to be honest with himself; he wasn't good at visiting. Keri had been right to call him out on that. Maybe he'd make this trip a yearly thing and return every Christmas. But maybe he wouldn't. So, he wanted to make the most of this visit. At least now he was here. So, he drove Uncle Frank to the senior center, where he was practicing for a ping-pong tournament.

"I don't need you to drive me," he grumbled.

"I know, but I don't have anything to do, so I can watch you play. Then we'll go get lunch. What you do you say?"

He grabbed his jacket, a hat, his gym bag, and headed to the car. "I want a burger."

"Okay, sounds good."

"I'm going to be there a while. If you want to go do something else for a while, go ahead."

"Funny, this is what I used to tell you when you'd take me to school or to baseball practice, remember?"

With a soft smile, Uncle Frank nodded. "Yeah, you didn't want an old man around when you were trying to look cool with all the girls."

Not really. The only girl he was interested in was Keri. "And now you don't want a handsome younger guy stealing all the older ladies away from you, is that it?"

Uncle Frank made a dismissive gesture, though when they got to the center, the older women did crowd around Frank and Jaden, cooing and patting his cheek, telling Uncle Frank they didn't know he had such a good-looking nephew.

Jaden raised an eyebrow as if to say, 'See what I told you?'

But his uncle looked proud and happy and bragged about what a successful and smart guy the boy was.

"Hey, would you mind helping me?" one lady asked Jaden. "I'm taking boxes down from the storage room to add more decorations, and they're kind of heavy."

"Don't hit on my nephew, Sarah," Uncle Frank said.

She playfully slapped his arm. "Oh, stop."

"I'd be happy to help. I can even help you decorate if you want. Uncle Frank, you go do your thing. I'm going to spend the morning with this beautiful woman."

Sarah blushed and laughed. Uncle Frank winked at him and told him to come to the back room when he finished to watch him whoop all the other guys.

Jaden followed Sarah to the crowded storage room and climbed on a ladder she provided to get three boxes down from the top shelf.

"Thank you so much. We got the tree ornaments down the other day and decorated the tree, but it's nicer when we can make the whole building look festive. Maybe even add a few strings of lights around the windows."

"Sure," Jaden said and carried the boxes back into the main room.

"I'm so glad you're here to visit your uncle. He may not have mentioned that he has developed neuropathy in his legs because of his diabetes. I worry about him sometimes."

"He hasn't told me." He hadn't even mentioned having diabetes.

"He has a lot of pain, and getting out of his chair at home can be difficult. I visit him a lot and make dinner for him, but he's so proud and independent."

Jaden opened the boxes, and together, they took the decorations out. "That's really kind of you."

"He's been so good to me. It's the least I can do."

Hmm, maybe Sarah and Uncle Frank were closer than they appeared. "I'll ask him about his legs and make sure he's getting the best treatment. Thank you for telling me."

She placed a hand on Jaden's cheek. "Of course, Sweetheart."

Keri walked into the senior center with her father, who complained about the cost of the repairs to his car, sharing that he might be better off buying another car if he was going to have to replace the engine. She felt a bit guilty declining Jaden's offer without allowing her father to speak for himself. And she was about to bring it up when she saw Jaden across the room.

Five senior women surrounded him, all talking to him, pointing to the wooden beams above their heads, and directing him to do something. He looked perfectly at home with all their attention. She couldn't help but smile.

Her father looked across the room, following her gaze. "Isn't that Jaden?"

"He seems to be everywhere these days," she said. Then she turned to her father. "Dad, I'm sorry I spoke for you about the car he wanted to give you. You can take it, you know. You don't have to spend all that money to buy a car if you can get one for free."

"Naw," he said. "He only offered it because he wanted to impress you."

"So? If the fool thinks he's going to buy my forgiveness, let him believe that."

"Let's see what the mechanic says about getting a replacement engine and what it will cost." He kissed her cheek. "Thanks for the ride. I'd better get back there. They're going to start the practice game without me."

As he headed down the hall to the back rooms, Keri strolled toward Jaden and the ladies.

"And if you can tape the garland," one said.

"But strings of lights would be so much better, don't you think?" another interrupted. "Is it hard to hang lights instead?"

"I imagine it would be a nightmare to get power up there, Helen," Sarah said.

"Ladies, why don't you leave it to me? I'll string lights where I can and decorate the beams with garland."

"And hang some round ornaments on the garland, too!"

He offered a charming smile. "Absolutely," he said as he noticed Keri watching them, and his smile grew. "Excuse me, Ladies."

"You're a regular Santa. Buying trees for your uncle. Putting decorations up here," Keri said.

"If some of my business associates could see me now, they'd never believe it. Or buy another car from me."

"Maybe they wouldn't, but I might."

"What?" He laughed. "In the market for a Rolls, after all?"

She shook her head. "The car you said you had for my dad. Is it in good condition? What kind of car is it?"

"Great condition. Almost new. It's a Lexus."

"A Lexus?" She had a hard time controlling her surprise or her voice. "You want to give my father a fifty-thousand-dollar car?"

"It's used. It's probably only worth twenty."

"Forget it. I can't afford that."

"Afford? I told you, it's a gift."

"A box of chocolates is a gift. A car is . . . a guilty conscience for abandoning me years ago?"

He placed a hand on his heart and tried to look hurt, but the humorous sparkle in his eyes ruined the effect. "First, a car, as you realize, is massively expensive, and I'm a smart businessman. I would not try to relieve my guilt, even with you, by losing money. This will benefit me in many ways. I'll outline them all if you want. And second, the gift is for your father, not for you."

She considered this. "Hmm, anyhow, it looks like his car is going to be beyond repair. He's going to need a replacement engine. Even a used one will cost him too much, and it might take weeks to get a new one if he goes that route. I was going to offer to buy your car."

He stepped forward and placed his hands on her shoulders. "I wish you weren't so stubborn or didn't assume my offer meant anything other than helping a family friend. It doesn't. But if you insist on buying it, okay. Give me a hundred bucks. It will look good on my books."

She shoved his hands off her. "Be serious."

"I'm serious."

"Give me a fair and reasonable price."

He sighed. "I can't charge you. I won't take your money."

For a second, she thought about it. Though she didn't want to get involved with him again, his gesture would help her father. And as he said, it had nothing to do with her, so she should step aside and let him do what he wanted. "I couldn't stop you from giving my dad a Christmas gift."

He lifted an eyebrow, and a corner grin appeared on his lips, reminding her of when they were teens and he'd had a sneaky idea. "You couldn't, could you?"

"What would it cost to get the car here?"

"Not much. I'd pay my employee to drive it here, so his time, plus gas."

If she accepted this offer from Jaden, she didn't want it to cost him additional money. He would already lose the car. "I'll pay for those costs. Fair?"

He thought about it for a second, then held out his hand. "Deal."

She shook his hand, and he gave it a couple of squeezes. "You make it hard for a guy to give you something."

"Wait, you're giving it to my dad. Not me. Right?"

"Absolutely," he said.

She gazed at the women who were watching them closely with the boxes of decorations at their feet, waiting patiently for his attention. Waving her hand around the room, she asked, "So, what are you doing here, Jaden?"

Looking over his shoulder, he said, "Oh, well, I drove my uncle here, and I...volunteered to help out. They're decorating for Christmas."

"They wrangled you into it, huh?"

"Naw. Well, sort of." He smiled. "I don't mind. I don't have anything else to do. A few million-dollar phone calls to make, but that's about it," he joked.

She held his gaze for a couple of seconds, then snapped out of it. "I need to get to work, but hey, thanks."

"I'll call Eduardo, and he'll have the car here in three days, tops."

"I'll write you a check for the cost. Let me know how much, okay?"

"Yep."

She took a couple of steps away, then turned back. "Can I ask you for another favor since you seem to be in a giving mood?"

He extended his arms out to his side as if he was open to anything. "I am definitely in the favor-granting mood."

She smiled. "When your uncle and my dad finish, would you mind dropping my dad off at home?" He doesn't have—."

"A car." He nodded.

"Right. And it will save my mom from having to come get him."

"You got it." Looking pleased with himself, he winked. "No problem at all."

Keri left owing Jaden way too much. She hoped she didn't come to regret it.

CHAPTER NINE

J aden considered himself fairly fit. He exercised regularly and went for runs a couple of times a week. But after putting up decorations at the senior center for three hours, he felt like he'd lifted weights for a week. It didn't help that his ribs still ached, and stretching his arms up to hang the garland and lights over his head felt like he was pulling his ribs apart.

But everything he did earned him excited exclamations of delight from the ladies, and he had to admit that their praise felt good. It was like having four adoring grandmothers pinching his cheeks and patting his head.

Of course, they didn't actually touch him, but the smiles and words of encouragement had the same effect. He even went out and bought additional lights and decorations to complement the ones they already had.

When he finished, they pumped sugar into his veins by offering him hot chocolate and cookies, which he gladly consumed as he watched them take pictures of his hard work.

He lay in bed the following morning until Uncle Frank pushed the door to his bedroom open. "You getting up today?"

"Those old women wore me out."

"I made some eggs and toast. Get up and eat."

Jaden pushed his way out of bed and walked slowly to the table wearing sweats and a t-shirt. Uncle Frank kept his house nice and warm.

"You mind if I ask you what's going on with that Keri girl?"

Jaden shoved some eggs into his mouth. "Mmm, good. What do you mean?" he said.

"Just that you went out to dinner with her, and Charles said you went to his house the other night with a bogus reason, saying you were going to give him a car."

Jaden laughed. "Why does everyone think it's bogus? I was serious. I want to give the man a car."

Frank pursed his lips and narrowed his eyes. "Get real, Jaden. What are you doing?"

"I went to his house to get Keri's address, I admit it, but then I decided to offer him a car I've been storing in my warehouse, taking up space. Seriously, he'd be doing me a favor, taking it off my hands."

"You mean to tell me you gave a stranger a car, but you didn't think to offer it to your uncle who raised you?"

Jaden almost choked on his coffee, half laughing. "You want a car, Uncle Frank?"

"That's not the point. If you were going to give a car away, wouldn't you give it to your family first?"

"You've never driven a sedan in your life, first of all. Second, you don't need car. Third, I'd buy you anything you wanted. You want a car?"

"Just think about what you're doing with that woman. She's not a teenager anymore, okay? And you're leaving in a couple of weeks."

Jaden finished his breakfast and stood at the sink to wash his plate, silverware, and cup. "Unbelievable. *You're* lecturing *me* about being fair to women? The king of broken hearts?"

"I never promised a woman anything I didn't deliver."

Jaden leaned on the counter by the sink and stared at his uncle. This was the first criticism he'd heard about him leaving the way he had, and it surprised him since he'd encouraged Jaden to go. "I'm not going to promise Keri anything. I'm just really trying to be nice to her, maybe make up for what I did to her. Am I trying to buy her forgiveness? Maybe, I don't know. But that doesn't make me a terrible guy, does it?

"No."

"That's all it is. Okay?"

"Okay."

"Plus, Mr. Anderson isn't a stranger. I dated his daughter for four years, and her parents always treated me like family. And you know I don't have many people that fall into that category."

Uncle Frank's face softened. "I know, Boy. I know." He stood unsteadily and added more coffee to his cup, then he sat and began scooping sugar from the sugar bowl into his coffee.

Jaden reached across and took the bowl away. "Try it without the sugar."

"What the hell?"

"That nice lady, Sarah, told me you have diabetes. You've never mentioned it."

"When was I supposed to mention it?" He shrugged. "I don't want to talk about that when you call. I want to hear how you're doing."

Jaden leaned on the counter and crossed his arms. "Maybe I want to know how *you're* doing, too."

"Now you know. No big deal."

Except that it is a big deal if he's having issues with his legs. "Well, do me a favor and cut the sugar, cut the carbs, okay? Keri's family is like family to me. You *are* family, and I want to keep you around."

Frank contemplated this and wouldn't meet Jaden's gaze, but he nodded. He took a sip of his coffee. "Ugh, taste like shit like this."

"You'll get used to it."

He grunted.

Jaden patted his uncle on the back. "I'm going to take a shower and rest to see if these ribs feel better."

That evening, Jaden called Eduardo and asked him to deliver the Lexus to Rapid City. "Bring my laptop too," he told him. Then they spoke about other business. Jaden still had the hope of moving one or possibly two cars before Christmas. Bethany Caroll was interested in his last Lamborghini, and Brandy Holden wanted the Bugatti La Voiture Noire. Both were shopping for their husbands. His next phone calls would be to them.

Eduardo agreed to leave the following morning. "Call Mrs. Holden though. She says that if she buys the Bugatti, she wants it sitting in her driveway Christmas morning."

"If she buys the Bugatti, I'll be there to cook her Christmas breakfast, walk her dogs, and do anything else she wants me to do. I'll call them both."

"Okay, I'll see you in a couple of days," Eduardo said.

Jaden booked Eduardo a return flight to California, then called the lovely ladies with the big wallets.

Once his fast-talking pitches were over, he was fairly sure Bethany would make a move on the car. She'd hinted to her husband about the car, and she said his eyes got dark and sexy when he thought about driving a Lamborghini. She'd let Jaden know soon.

Brandy was a little more iffy. Her husband had so many cars. Would adding a Bugatti to his collection really impress a man who had "a bunch" already? Jaden had to explain that this was not just any car. Yes, it would impress him. Collectors wanted the best of the best. But he was performing his Christmas specials in Europe, and she was angry that she hadn't been invited to go with him. "He's probably sleeping with a different woman every night," she said.

Jaden sat on his bed, legs crossed, holding his forehead. These women! "Come on, Brandy. You know how much he loves you. It's the Christmas season. People love to go to Christmas concerts. He's doing his job."

Jaden spent thirty minutes playing therapist, and finally, she said she'd let him know about the car.

He ended the call and dropped the phone on his bed. Hell, he needed a drink.

Voices from the living room filtered into his bedroom. A woman's voice. Uncle Frank had a visitor. Should he stay in his bedroom or go out there? Curiosity won, and he stood and left the bedroom. Sarah sat with her uncle, chatting away.

When she saw him, her face lit up. "Jaden!" She stood and pulled him into a hug.

"Good to see you."

"I dropped by with a pot roast and mashed potatoes for you boys."

Jaden rubbed his stomach. "Yum. Thank you."

"I hope you don't mind that I redecorated your bedroom. I tried to update it to a mature room, but keep your personality, history, and mood."

So, she was the woman who did the decorating. "You did an amazing job! It needed updating." It was no longer "his" room, but he didn't want to mention that since she was so proud and obviously wanted to impress him.

She blushed. "I'm glad you like it."

"I say we eat," Uncle Frank said.

They moved to the kitchen and ate the delicious meal she had brought. After, she insisted on doing the dishes before she went home.

Uncle Frank sank into his chair, complaining about how full he was the second she walked out of the door. He'd been super charming while Sarah had been here.

"Me too," Jaden said. "She's a nice lady."

"Yes, she's wonderful."

"She seems to like you. She told me that you helped her out with something."

"Ah yes, she was going to lose her home because she couldn't afford the property taxes that increased with the value of her home. Her asshole son planned to take advantage of her situation and basically kick her out of her house by moving her into a state facility and 'taking over' her property tax payments. I helped her apply for a property tax refund that seniors can qualify for, and I paid her taxes for that year."

This touched Jaden's heart. "Her son was a total jerk. Classy move, Uncle Frank."

"No big deal."

"That pot roast says it was a big deal to her."

"Yeah." The warm look in his eyes gave away how much he cared about his friend. He flipped on the TV, which meant the conversation was over. Jaden settled into the cushions of the couch, put his feet up on the coffee table, and enjoyed being in the room with his uncle.

CHAPTER TEN

As Keri finished with her last customer, Jaden called to say that his friend had delivered her dad's car and asked if he could come over to show it to her. He sounded so excited.

For the past three days, he'd stayed out of her way as promised, which she appreciated. "I'll be closing in about thirty minutes. Do you want to meet me at my place in about an hour and fifteen minutes?"

"Great, see you soon."

She turned to the lady holding a couple of reindeer candleholders. "Did you decide on these?"

"I really like them, but I'm flying to Albuquerque, and I'm afraid they'll break on the trip."

"I can ship them. I pack things nice and snug, and you'd have them in a couple of days."

The woman turned them over in her hands and couldn't seem to make up her mind.

"If you want them. No pressure," Keri said.

"I think I'll take them in my carry-on bags. They'll be okay, right?"

Keri shrugged and smiled. "It's up to you."

The woman took out her credit card, and her husband, waiting by the door, breathed a sigh of relief. He appeared to have been tired of waiting forty-five minutes ago, but he patiently sat on the bench that Keri had placed close to the Christmas tree. Sometimes, people liked to pose their kids and take pictures of them sitting in front of the trees.

Once the couple left, Keri turned off the Christmas music, cleaned up, totaled her sales, and dropped cash in her bank bag. She put on her jacket, hat, and gloves. Turning her lights off and locking her door, she wondered if she had time to grab some food before heading home. Probably not.

She drove home in the dark, enjoying the Christmas lights and holiday music. This was still her favorite time of year. Magic seemed to permeate the air.

She stopped at her parent's house and picked Mochi up. As always, he was excited to see her, and after running in circles in the front yard, he hopped into her truck. When she got to her apartment, Jaden was leaning against her door waiting for her. A huge box was also propped up for her outside her door.

"Hi," she said, noticing that the box was from the sperm bank. She had her first appointment in a couple of days, so she was glad it arrived in the promised overnight shipment.

"Want me to bring this in?" he asked.

"Oh, okay, thanks."

Mochi jumped on him, and he laughed. "Hello, buddy. How have you been?" He picked up the box and carried it inside her house, leaning it against the wall in her entry. "Heavy."

Her face warmed. "Yeah. It's for my science experiment." She walked into the kitchen to get Mochi's dinner ready. "Can I get you anything? Water? Coffee?"

"No, thanks. Science experiment?" He glanced at the shipping label.

"I'm kidding." She opened a can of dog food.

"What's a cryobank?" Jaden asked.

She studied him for a few seconds. "Promise not to tell a soul?"

"Tell them what? And who would I tell?"

"I'm going to have a procedure done to try to get pregnant. And that is the sperm I'm going to need."

His eyes widened. "You're kidding again, right?"

She picked up Mochi's bowl and added a scoop of dry food, then emptied the can of beef and gravy. Mochi barked excitedly. She placed the bowl on the kitchen floor, and he quieted down. Keri leaned across the counter. "I'm serious. I've decided I want to have a baby."

He moved closer and took a seat on one of her barstools. "But why this way? I mean, why not get married or, you know, do it with a guy?"

"Do it?" She smirked. "Really?"

"Get pregnant, I mean, Keri. You don't even know who the father will be."

"The father won't be anyone. The baby will just have me. It's not ideal, but I'm not getting any younger, and I really want to be a mom."

He seemed truly shocked. "I didn't know women really did these things."

"This woman is going to."

He raised an eyebrow. "Well, you're full of surprises. You must have thought about this a lot?"

"I have. Remember, don't say anything to anyone. Not my parents. Not my friends. It might not work, so I'm keeping it quiet for now."

He studied her and shrugged. "Why tell me?"

"You're kind of a ghost. You'll be gone soon. And you don't really care about me."

"Ouch, that's not true."

"I mean, like my parents who would worry and freak out, or my friends who would try to talk me out of it and tell me to wait."

He stood. "Yeah, you're right, I wouldn't do either of those things. I hope it works the way you want it to. You deserve to be happy, Keri."

"Thanks." She came around the bar. "Should we go see the car? I'm excited." Mochi had finished eating and would need to go out, but he could wait a few minutes.

Jaden nodded, and they headed back outside. He led her to a sleek black Lexus sedan and told her to get inside. "You want to drive it?"

"No, you drive."

As they headed down West Blvd and out to Omaha, she enjoyed the smooth ride. "Oh my God, my Dad is going to love this."

"I hope so."

"Jaden, are you sure about this? Let me make payments. If you want to be nice, sell it to me for half off. Even at ten thousand, you're giving us an amazing deal, and I can afford that."

"We had a deal. Don't back out now. You owe me a few hundred for gas to get it here, a thousand for Eduardo's time, and four hundred for his airline ticket back to California."

"Okay. I'll write you a check when we get back to the apartment."

He appeared to like her answer. "Want some food? We can pick up some fast food and take it back to your place."

"Yes! I'm starving."

Jaden went through Arby's drive-thru, buying roast beef sandwiches, fries, and cokes. He carried it all up to her apartment, trying not to notice her backside as she climbed the stairs. She'd blown him away with her secret.

He wasn't sure how he felt about her getting purposely pregnant with some random guy's sperm. Not that it was any of his business, but hell, what a crazy decision to make. He'd never understand women.

"Down, Mochi," she said as they entered her living room. She turned the lights on and sat on the carpet by a coffee table. "Let's eat here. It's more comfortable than the barstools."

He placed the bags down and sat beside her. She dug into the food immediately.

Watching her, he couldn't help but smile. "Hungry?"

"Starving. I haven't eaten anything all day. Eat," she encouraged.

Mochi curled into his bed, sighed, and closed his eyes.

Jaden reached for his hot, cheesy sandwich. "How are we going to approach the idea of the car with your dad? You agreed, but he never did."

"Good question." She ate a few fries. "He's a proud man. Let me think about it for a day or two."

He reached into his pocket and pulled out the keys. Smiling, he held them out to her.

She reached for them, and he took her hand, holding it for a second before placing the keys in the palm of her hand and closing her fingers around them. "It's good to be with you again after all these years, Keri," he said, wanting to say so much more. "I forgot how good it felt to be close to you."

In a split second, her warm and easy expression turned into a hard mask, and her eyes became devoid of any warmth. "Go to hell." She eased her hand back and looked down at her lap, appearing uncomfortable now that he'd touched her. He shouldn't have, but he couldn't help himself. Being with her again, hanging out like they used to felt so good.

His uncle's warnings came back to him, and his own desire to make things right and not screw up again told him it was time to go. He pushed his food back, scooping it into his bag.

"I really hate you," she said.

He nodded.

"I'm serious."

"I know. I believe you." He got on his knees to leave, but she reached over and pushed him back hard, making him fall on his butt. "Ugh, damn it, my ribs."

Mochi raised his head and growled. Keri patted his head, and thankfully, the dog didn't pounce on Jaden. He lowered his head but didn't close his eyes.

"Where are you going? Running away, Jaden?"

Cradling his side, he scooted back to lean on her couch. "Seemed like you wanted me to leave."

"I want to yell at you."

"Okay."

"I want to tell you how much I hate you for leaving, and for coming back and acting like we're old friends, and for giving my dad a car, and shit, for being in my house and . . . and making me forget that I hate you."

He ran a hand through his hair and waited to see if she had finished. "Do you want to hit me again?"

She stared at him. A flush spread across her features, and the tension that had existed just moments before faded, replaced with a tiny smile that turned into laughter. "No, I don't want to hit you." She moved closer. "Are you okay?" She kept laughing. "You look scared."

"I'm a little scared."

She continued to chuckle, and then she threw a fry at him. "I'm going to write you a check. Then you're going to leave," she said. "And once this 'deal' between us is over, you're going to stay away from me. Got it?"

He picked up the fry and threw it back at her. "What if I don't want to?"

Now she leaned in really close, studying him, almost like she was going to kiss him. "If you don't stay away from me, I will make you fall in love with me again, and it won't be good for you."

Swallowing, he placed a hand on her shoulder, sliding his fingers up her neck and into her hair. "It won't?"

"It will be humiliating."

Jaden had two major faults. The first was that he couldn't resist a challenge. The second was that he never did what he was supposed to do. Still, he got on his knees, determined to leave, but she didn't back up, so instead of dropping his hand, he cupped the back of her head and took her lips, kissing her like he'd wanted to since he'd first seen her at the Christmas tree lot. A cautious, exploratory kiss, searching for something . . . the past maybe, memories, and forgotten needs.

And she allowed herself to explore along with him. Her hands at first gripped his shoulders, but then they caressed his face and head. She moaned and deepened the kiss, opening her mouth, her tongue dancing with his, and he could feel this getting out of control. Right before he was about to pull her closer, she pushed back. "Oh shit," she said.

Drawing in a breath, he watched her try to get control of her own breathing, and he wanted to reach for her again before she managed it. He knew this could go further tonight. And he wanted it to, but for the first time ever, he decided not to push his luck. Not with Keri. He would not hurt her again. "This wasn't what I intended to do tonight."

"What?" she asked.

Had he said that out loud? "I didn't mean to do that, Keri?"

With a nervous laugh, she shrugged.

He stood, grabbed his bag of food, and tossed it into the kitchen trash can. Then he snatched his jacket and hat and gazed at her. "You win. I'll stay away from you." He walked out her door and ran downstairs. Only when he got to the bottom did he realize he needed her to give him a ride home. "Fuck." He climbed back up and banged on her door.

She opened it, and they stared at each other. Her lips were wet and bright red. Her cheeks brushed in an attractive pink, her eyes wide, and her pupils enlarged as if she were alert and preparing for an attack from a predator or simply aroused.

He groaned inwardly. "I drove the car here. I need a ride."

Reaching up, she caressed his face gently as if finally recognizing him. The tenderness was the opposite of the angry attack from a few minutes ago. He wanted so badly for her to pull him inside and tell him to stay, that she forgave him, that she wanted him.

But she took a step back, put on her jacket and beanie, and grabbed her purse. "Stay Mochi. I'll be back," she said as she locked her door and hurried downstairs to her truck.

She drove without speaking. The tension buzzed between them like an overloaded electrical circuit.

"Christmas used to be my favorite time of year, but once you left, it was a long time before I could enjoy it again." She pulled her truck up his uncle's driveway and stopped to let him out. "The holidays just brought back that empty feeling of not being wanted."

"Awe, Keri." He reached across and ran the back of his fingers down her cheek. "If you don't hear anything else I've said, please know that it wasn't you."

"You left *me*."

"I left. Looking for me."

She nodded. "And did you find what you were looking for, Jade?"

She used the shortened version of his name, the one she used when they were friends and lovers and so close that they told each other everything. "I don't know anymore. In some ways. But I also left part of myself here. I'm realizing this now."

"I guess there are always trade-offs." Tears glistened in her eyes.

"I guess so." But at this very second, having traded her for money and success made him feel like the biggest idiot in the world. His stomach physically ached.

With nothing left to say, she looked out her front windshield, and it was his cue to leave. He got out, closed the door, and held his hand up as she backed out.

CHAPTER ELEVEN

Jaden didn't sleep well. His mind kept replaying that kiss and what he could have done differently both last night and ten years ago. Though he regretted his past actions, he didn't regret last night's kiss. Her lips were as soft as he remembered, but the years of maturity had made her less hesitant, and way more tempting. At least a dozen times during the night, as he tossed and turned, he told himself that he should not start anything with Keri. She was off limits. But he wasn't sure he'd convinced himself.

When he got up in the morning, he stumbled into the bathroom and got in the shower. He stood there as the hot water massaged his head and woke him up. He rubbed his face and soaped his body. Looking down at his erection, he groaned. This was what he got for thinking of Keri all night long. Damned fool. He turned the water to cold. Rinsed off, then shivered as he toweled himself dry.

After the shower, he started feeling somewhat alive and more awake, but what he really needed was coffee. In the kitchen, he poured himself a full cup and noticed a note on the refrigerator from his uncle. He had gone to work.

"Work?" He'd retired a couple of years ago from the wastewater treatment facility in Spearfish. Where was he working now?

On the fridge, his uncle also had a work list for things he needed to do around the house. He'd always kept his To-do list for himself and for Jaden under a magnet of a sexy woman who said, "You want to impress me? Do it fast." He thought it was a hilarious magnet to hold a To-do list even though more than one of his female friends told him it was inappropriate, especially with a young boy in the house. But Uncle Frank never took it down.

Jaden noticed that one item on his list was to replace two window well covers. Glancing out of the kitchen window at the cold and snow on the ground as he sipped his coffee in the warm house, Jaden wasn't sure if this was a good time to replace anything outside. But he put on a jacket and slipped into his uncle's work boots. He circled the house and bent down to look at the cracked covers that were probably allowing melted snow and water to leak into the windows.

Returning to the house, he entered the garage to see if Uncle Frank had already purchased the replacement covers, but he couldn't find any.

This was something he could do for his uncle, so he grabbed his keys, drove to Ace Hardware, and bought two elongated window well covers that would protect the windows completely.

Strolling through the store, whistling along to the Christmas music, Jaden found he was enjoying checking out all the cool stuff. He didn't have time to do this in Los Angeles. In fact, he couldn't remember the last time he'd been in a home improvement store. When something broke in his house, he called someone to fix it.

As he headed to the checkout lane, he remembered the hand saw he wanted to buy to replace the old one Frank had. He found a nice fifteen-inch one and added it to his cart.

Back at Uncle Frank's house, he grabbed the tools he needed and quickly replaced both covers. He admired his work for a second or two, then carried the old ones and dropped them into the trash cans.

Grateful to be finished, he went back inside to get warm and put the tools away. In the garage, he saw a box that had his mother's name. Out of curiosity, he pulled it down and opened it. Inside were random things. Hair bows, picture frames of people–teens, he didn't know, a high school yearbook, a picture of her and Dad when they were young, a journal. He picked up the journal and saw from the dates that she'd probably written in it when she was in middle and high school. "Hmm," he said without reading any of it and closed it. There was a medal she'd won playing volleyball, a Mickey Mouse statue, a cup with the name of her college, and a little rattle with the name Jaden. She'd also kept his handprint pressed into plaster.

He smiled and, for another second, stared at the collection of things before closing the box and placing it back on the shelf. He then went back inside the house and lay on the couch, staring at the white ceiling, remembering how angry he'd been at his parents for dying and leaving him. Now, he thought about how sad it was that their lives full of unfulfilled dreams had been cut short.

The front door opened.

Uncle Frank scoffed. "Look at you. Get your lazy ass up and roll my trash cans to the curb, will you? The trash truck comes tonight."

Jaden grinned. "Sure, Uncle Frank." He stood. "Where are you working? And why?"

"I have a part-time job selling tickets at the Monument. It keeps me busy, and sometimes I get to watch free concerts or attend sporting events."

The Monument was a large exhibition center. Jaden used to go there to watch hockey games, but the center also hosted major concerts, job fairs, and other events.

Uncle Frank groaned as he sat in his chair. "The Nutcracker ballet will be playing for the next few days, and they needed extra help, so I went, but my legs are killing me."

Jaden felt bad for his uncle. "Let's make an appointment to see a doctor soon. Maybe there's something they can do."

"I've seen doctors, Boy. They've done what they can. Cleaning up my diet will help. I'm working on it."

"Okay. I'll go get those trash cans. Anything else I can do?"

He shook his head.

Jaden put his jacket and the boots back on and returned outside. Maybe he'd make a salad for them to share, and he'd ask him about his mother's box. Or maybe he wouldn't. Uncle Frank had obviously found it in his parents' home when he cleaned it out to sell it, and he decided to keep his mother's mementos. Jaden had never considered how painful it had been for him to lose his sister. As a boy, Jaden had only thought about what *he'd* lost. He was a kid, after all, a seven-year-old kid.

When he got back inside, he leaned down and kissed his uncle on the top of his head.

"What the hell's that for?"

"I love you, Uncle Frank."

A frown drew his eyebrows together. "Are you okay?"

"Yeah."

"Okay." He turned back to his TV, but he didn't turn it on. "I'm glad you came to visit me, you know? I've missed seeing you."

Jaden sat across from him on the couch and nodded. "I've missed you too. I'm sorry for disappearing." His eyes grew moist, and the image of his uncle blurred. "I've been an awful nephew and boyfriend and friend. I don't like the guy you all see."

Uncle Frank cleared his throat. "Hey," he said in a gruff tone. "I see a good man who has built a business out of nothing, who works hard, who is successful. I see a generous man. I used to see a boy, but now I see a man, Jaden."

He stared down at his feet and nodded. He blinked his eyes rapidly. "Thanks. When I lived here, I wanted to be someone else so bad, you know?

I don't know why. People loved me here the way I was. I guess I didn't get it. How could they love a poor, orphan kid with no future?"

Uncle Frank leaned forward and tapped the side of Jaden's face. It felt like three short slaps.

Jaden raised his gaze. They sat there in silence.

Uncle Frank raised an eyebrow. "You're still the same person everyone loved. You're still my boy."

Jaden nodded, touched. Uncle Frank had never dared to call Jaden his. It was always 'my sister's kid' or my nephew. He swallowed the lump in his throat. "I changed your window well covers," he said.

"Oh yeah?" He eased back into his chair. "Thanks."

"I'll go make us some salads."

"I don't like salad."

"Too bad. Learn to like it." Jaden stood. "If there's nothing else the doctors can do, then it's up to you."

"Fine. Add onions."

The Friday night ping-pong tournament had finally arrived, and Keri's parents were excited. To be more precise, it was her father who was excited. He'd been talking about it for days and practiced on his dining table, driving her mother crazy.

Since the participants' families were invited to the senior center to watch the competition and enjoy Christmas goodies, Keri promised to close the store early and pick them up in time for them all to arrive a few minutes early.

Her mother agreed to feed Mochi and to walk him to save time, so when she pulled up to their house, they were wrapped up in their warm coats and waiting. They ran through the wind and hopped in the car, her mom in the front and her father in the back.

"That dog recognizes the sound of your car. He ran to the door when you pulled up."

"Awe, poor guy."

"He's spoiled rotten. I walked him, fed him a home-cooked meal, and gave him milk bones for his teeth."

"Thanks, Mom. What would I do without you?" Part of her wondered if her mother would be willing to do the same with her baby if she got pregnant. Was it fair to plan to have a child without discussing it with them first? In some ways, it would impact them too. If the insemination worked, she'd let them know immediately.

The quick ten-minute drive allowed her mother to fill Keri in on all the senior center gossip. Mom didn't go often, though she enjoyed her aerobics class.

The instant they entered the vast open room, Keri was captivated and couldn't believe her eyes. The center employees and volunteers had turned the lights down low, and the room glittered with fake snowflakes, colorful blinking lights, and Christmas balls hanging from the ceiling. There were also a couple of extra small trees. Kelly Clarkson's "Please Come Home for Christmas" played through the speakers.

"Wow," she said. "It's like Christmas Wonderland in here."

The volunteer beamed as she greeted everyone at the door. "Yes, isn't it amazing? Frank's nephew stayed here for hours getting it all up the other day. He even went out and bought extra garlands and lights and a couple of small trees. And today, he brought gifts for all the volunteers and placed them under the tree."

Santa strikes again. He really was in a giving mood.

"It's perfectly festive," her mother said.

"Mesmerizing," Keri agreed.

"I'm going to go warm up my arm," her father said. "They're going to turn on the lights soon, I hope."

"Oh, yes, we only have them low until everyone arrives to create atmosphere, you know, Charles."

As he hurried off, Keri led her mother to the food and drinks table. Keri drank 7-up and pretended it was something more exciting. She took in the room again, and as she did, she noticed Jaden sitting on a stool on the other side of the room. He was watching her.

She held up her cup and waved an arm at the room, mouthing a silent "wow."

He laughed.

Keri strolled with her mother until her mom found her friends. "I'm going to go find us some seats so we can watch the game," Keri said.

She purposely did not sit on the same side as Jaden, which maybe was silly, but after the other night's wild kiss, which had kept her awake half the night, she needed to stay away from him. He said he hadn't meant to kiss her, but she didn't believe him. He'd wanted to, and she'd wanted him to, and he had. And now it was over.

So, instead of sitting next to each other, they sat on opposite sides and stared at each other. Then she'd look away and eventually look back and find him watching her, but immediately, he'd look up at the ceiling. Finally, they both smiled, and he stood and walked around the ping-pong tables and took a seat beside her.

"Hi," he said.

"Hi."

"I couldn't help but notice you staring at me."

"Shut up." She elbowed him with a laugh, but he clenched his teeth in pain. "Oh, I'm so sorry. I keep forgetting about your bruised ribs." She placed a hand on his forearm.

"No more stupid pickup lines for you. Even as a joke."

"I'm sorry." She caressed his arm for a second, then pulled back. "You went all out, Father Christmas. It's gorgeous in here."

"You like it? It got me major brownie points with the senior ladies. My uncle was jealous."

"They will probably all adopt you."

"If it means home-cooked meals, I'll take it. Sarah brought us some delicious pot roast, but I think it's because she has the hots for my uncle."

Keri had always been amused by Jaden's uncle. "Women always have, haven't they?"

"It runs in the family."

She raised an eyebrow, not really wanting to know about all of Jaden's conquests.

But he chuckled. "Not that I've ever taken advantage of my natural good looks like my uncle has."

"You're full of shit," she said.

Soon, the lights came on, and the Christmas music was turned down. The evening host quieted everyone and explained the rules of the game and how the teams would compete.

"This is serious," Jaden whispered in her ear.

Keri fought back a smile. "Shh."

Her mother sat beside her. She waved at Jaden. He leaned across Keri and kissed her mother on the cheek.

"There are three players per team," the speaker informed the audience. "The winning team must win three individual matches. We have four teams. Can each of the teams stand as I introduce you? Hold your applause until they are all standing."

"She must have been in the military," he whispered again.

Keri widened her eyes. "Quiet."

"I should have brought coffee. This is going to take a while."

This time, she nodded.

But once the games began, it became clear that it wasn't going to take very long at all. Ping Pong balls flew everywhere as the players swung wildly with their paddles, and the opposing team missed returning them. The audience laughed and joked. Both sides racked up points quickly.

All three of them cheered for both Frank and for her father, even though they played against each other.

"Traitors," her father called out jokingly, pointing his paddle at Keri and her mother.

For the next two hours, they had the most fun Keri had had in a long time. Laughing, oohing and awing, clapping, and even standing up and cheering when either her father or Frank missed a ball after many successful hits. Finally, her father failed to return the ball, losing to Frank who made a big deal about beating him.

"He needs to learn how to win gracefully," Jaden said, making a cringy face.

"They love to tease each other," Keri's mother said.

After the game, Keri heard her name and saw Amanda waving at her. "Oh my God," she said and crossed the room. "What are you doing here? Have you been here the whole time?"

"Yeah, I came to watch my grandfather play. And, of course, you didn't see me. You and Jaden are looking pretty chummy. You guys can't keep your hands off each other."

Keri laughed. "We were just enjoying the game. His uncle played my dad."

Amanda gave her a 'yeah right' look.

"This is what I'm supposed to be doing, remember? Making him fall for me so I can dump him." She wasn't sure why she said that, except that maybe admitting that she was enjoying being with Jaden made her feel too much like the fool she'd been as a teenager. Fool me once and all that.

"Well, it looks like it's working. He's all over you."

"Yeah," Keri said, wanting to change the subject. "What time is Jenn having Brady's birthday party on Sunday?"

"Five." She lifted her chin. "Lover boy is coming in for the kill."

Keri looked over her shoulder and groaned inside. Apparently, they'd both completely forgotten the decision to stay away from each other.

"Hey, sorry to interrupt. I just wanted to say bye."

"Jaden, you remember Amanda."

"Of course," he said, reaching to shake her hand. "We used to fight for Keri's attention back in high school, too."

Amanda grinned. "No fighting. She's all yours."

"Are you leaving already? I mean, doesn't your uncle want to socialize, have some snacks, and brag about his big win?" Keri asked.

"He's tired, and his legs hurt. Too much exertion for one night. But you want to do the car thing tomorrow."

"I can't. I have a doctor's appointment."

He frowned. "Oh, Oh! Right. Well, I hope everything goes well. Maybe Sunday?"

"I'll call you."

He nodded, said goodbye to Amanda, and left.

Amanda raised an eyebrow. "Okay, seriously, what's going on?"

Keri shrugged. "It's a long story, but the short version is he's giving my dad a car because his old Ford Fusion broke down, and it's not worth repairing it. It's a surprise, so don't say anything."

"Be careful, Keri."

"I am. Don't worry."

"I do. He's too slick, too charming, too temporary."

"And I'm glad. I have zero interest in him."

But as they left the room where he'd dominated her attention, mystified her with his ability to think of simple ways to make people happy, and overwhelmed her senses with color, lights, and smells of Christmas, could she really continue to say she wasn't just a little interested? If she was honest, just being in the same room with him seemed to make her happy and feel alive, which meant she'd learned nothing in ten years.

CHAPTER TWELVE

Keri wrung her fingers as she waited in the cold exam room at the clinic, wrapped in a paper gown. The nurse had taken her temperature and blood pressure and prepared all the instruments for the insemination.

By the time the doctor arrived, Keri was a nervous wreck.

Her gynecologist slipped on her blue latex gloves, as did her nurse.

"It's a simple procedure. You won't feel much," Doctor Pruitt reassured her. "You'll lay there for about twenty minutes, then go home, and pray for the best."

"It sounds so simple for something that can change my entire life."

Doctor Pruitt agreed. "It's always simple. One drink. One night. And then a lifetime of someone calling you Mom." She patted Keri's knee. "That's what you want, though, right?"

"Yes. I'm just a little scared. What if I am making a mistake?"

"You can still back out."

Keri thought about it and shook her head. "No, I'd always wonder if I should have done it." And being in her thirties and forties without at least one child would make her feel truly miserable and her life feel purposeless.

The doctor nodded. "Okay, lie back, relax, and think of the baby you want. You might feel a little cramping because I'm inserting the syringe into the uterus."

She asked her nurse to hand her the instruments she needed. There was a slight discomfort, but it didn't hurt, and she didn't cramp. Doctor Pruitt was gentle.

In the midst of performing the procedure, the doctor mentioned to the nurse the phone consultation she had scheduled before her lunch break and how much she was looking forward to the basil chicken and rice leftovers she'd made the night before.

It struck Keri as surreal that these two women were having a casual conversation about lunch while Keri was on her back being inseminated. She supposed anything could become routine if you did it every day. But this experience wasn't routine for her. She felt awkward and couldn't wait for it to be over.

And it was. Very quickly. Before Keri could form another thought, Doctor Pruitt stood. "There we go," she said. "All done." Both the doctor and nurse wished her luck and told her to stay put until they instructed her to leave.

She lay there alone, and tears filled her eyes. Having a baby and getting pregnant was supposed to be a result of being in love, of planning with the guy of your dreams. She imagined telling her husband and hugging each other, so excited about becoming parents together.

The problem was that there was never a face to accompany that dream of hers. The man beside her was a ghost. And immediately, that thought made her think of Jaden. She shook her head. No, she didn't want to think of him, especially not right now.

At exactly twenty minutes, the nurse opened the door to let her know that she was free to get dressed now.

"Are you sure? I don't want to mess anything up."

The nurse kindly assured Keri she couldn't mess anything up, but if she wanted to stay a little longer, she could. Keri stayed another ten minutes, then she got up and got dressed. She drove straight home, where she crawled into bed and cried into her pillow.

Jaden cleared trash away from his uncle's yard. He'd stacked old paint cans and other junk on the side of the garage to take to the dump. Jaden placed them in the trunk of his uncle's car. He could get rid of it all later.

For some reason, he felt the need to keep his mind off of Keri and what she was doing today. He felt like running into that medical office and telling her not to do it. If she wanted sperm, he'd donate his. He didn't want a kid, but if she wanted one so badly that she bought a stranger's DNA, he could offer his. At least she knew Jaden; they had a history together. And Jaden could help her pay for the kid and even visit sometimes. She wouldn't have to tell the kid that he was the father. He could just be the cool friend.

He carried firewood into the house. "What the fuck am I thinking? I've lost it." The last thing he needed was to get involved in a woman's crazy plan to make a baby.

Jaden placed the firewood by the fireplace, and Frank built the fire. Jaden sank into his uncle's comfortable couch to enjoy watching a college bowl game. But before halftime, his phone rang, and he saw that it was Keri. For a second, he considered not answering. Let her go, he told himself. He'd apologized, bought her a nice meal, and even kissed her when he shouldn't have. There was nothing left for him to do or say. "Excuse me," he said to Uncle Frank and closed the door to his bedroom to take the call.

"Hey," he said.

"I told you I'd call about the car," she said, sounding tired or maybe sad.

Right. The car. "Do you want to give it to your dad on your own? Do you need me to be there?"

"I don't need you to be there, but since you're giving it to him."

He sat on his bed, the old springs creaking and popping under him. He imagined the coils rubbing together. "Tell him it's from you."

"I can't do that. But if you don't want to be there . . ."

"No, no, I want to be there." He pinched the bridge of his nose. "Tomorrow?"

"Sure. My friend Jenn is having a birthday party for one of her kids at five in the afternoon. Do you want to meet at four?"

"Okay."

"Okay," she said, but didn't hang up. "See you at my parent's place, then."

Should he ask? No, no he shouldn't, but he said, "You okay?" He looked across the room at her framed photo.

"I'm in bed, hiding under my covers."

He didn't want to picture her in bed. "Why?"

"The procedure today. Just calling it a procedure is depressing. I suppose I should be happy, but I'm not. I don't know. I feel weird."

"It's a weird thing."

Her musical laughter made him happy he hadn't hung up. "Men don't think of doing things like that. It's hard for me to relate."

"You never thought of having kids?"

"Naw. Though I don't have anything against them." He'd honestly make a terrible father, worse than his uncle, because at least his uncle had a stable home for Jaden.

"Well, that's good."

"I mean, I like them, but I never stopped to consider making my own. I haven't had a lifestyle that would be good for kids, you know. I'm always traveling, attending events, working late. I can't imagine myself with a kid."

"And I've watched all my friends get married and have kids. So, I'm feeling like I'm behind."

"It's not a race."

"No, but women have a limited window to have children, and then it's over. You, meaning men, can wait until you're eighty. But it's not the same for women."

"Being a woman sucks."

She laughed again. "Why am I talking to you?"

He stretched back into bed and looked out his window at the gorgeous scenery. "Hell if I know. It's a first for me, I'll tell you that much. Babies. Artificial Insemination. I'm out of my depth. But I'm happy to listen and make stupid jokes."

"I think I'll just see you tomorrow."

He smiled. "Okay, Keri. And hey."

"Hmm."

"Once you're holding that kid, you won't remember how it was created. Smile, okay?"

The line was quiet for a second. "That's the kindest thing you've ever said to me, Jaden," she said.

Once they hung up, he sat there for a few minutes. Damn it, why did he have the urge to go see her, to hold her, and to do anything necessary to make sure she had a smile on her face?

CHAPTER THIRTEEN

K eri pulled up to her parent's house with the Lexus, and a few seconds later, Jaden joined her. He climbed out of his car and strolled
toward her, looking relaxed and healthier than he had in days. She probably
shouldn't notice how he filled out a pair of jeans like a fashion model. He'd
gotten more muscular with age, and the denim molded tightly to his thighs.
They rode low on his hips, defining and hugging him in all the right places.

"How you doin'?" he asked as she reached her side.

Pulling her attention away from his body, she smiled. "Good. But not
sure how this is going to go. Shall we?"

"Hold on a sec." He ran back to his car, pulled out a massive red bow,
and attached it to the hood of the car.

"That's perfect," she said.

"It's all in the presentation." He winked and waved a hand toward the
door, not looking stressed at all.

Keri unlocked the door and entered her parent's home with Jaden right behind her. If her mother was surprised to see them together, she didn't show it. "Well, hi you two. Did you bring the dog?"

"No, he should be fine by himself for a little while."

Her dad was watching TV in the living room. He stood when he saw them come in. "I didn't know you were stopping by today. Your mother said you had a party to go to."

"I do. But I wanted to bring Jaden by first. He has something to tell you."

Her father raised an eyebrow, and she realized that sounded kind of odd. But Jaden quickly stepped in. "Actually, I was wondering if you would come outside with me for a minute. I want to show you something. You too, Mrs. Anderson."

"You both are acting strange tonight," she said, but her parents headed to the front door and grabbed their coats off the hooks in the entry.

When they got to the porch, her father noticed the car parked on the street immediately. He turned to Jaden and said, "Don't tell me this is the car you've been wanting to give me."

"Yes, sir. I just want you to see it, and I want you to consider it a Christmas gift as a thank you for all the times you've welcomed me into your home."

"Come on, Daddy. Let's go take a look. Mom?" she said, widening her eyes and waving her mother forward to encourage her to support this.

Her father looked at her. "Didn't you tell him we were absolutely not going to accept this?"

"He convinced me that it was the right thing to do."

"It's a gift from the two of us, sir. Keri pitched in, so it's not really free."

Now, her father frowned. "You can't afford to spend money on a car for me. I can buy my own car, Keri."

"I only paid to get it transported here, which seemed fair."

"I should pay for that," he said. "What am I saying? I can't accept this, Jaden."

"Will you look at it first? It's a nice car, Dad. And you said yourself that you don't need a new car and don't want the payments."

"Come on, honey," her mother said, leading her father to the curb. "Let's just look at it. They went to all the trouble to get it here."

Keri glanced at Jaden, and he smiled. They followed the older couple to the curb. Jaden told him about the miles on the car, the maintenance that had been done, and that he had the title in the name of his business. "You'd have to pay for the new registration, of course," Jaden said. "I'm going to write up the bill of sale for what Keri is paying."

Her father nodded as he examined the beautiful car.

Keri gave her mother the keys. "Take it for a ride or at least sit in it, Mom."

Her mother encouraged her father to get inside. He started the car and pulled away from the curb.

"Our job is done," Jaden said with a grin.

"I don't know. You think I'm stubborn. My dad is even more so."

Jaden shoved his hands in his jeans pockets and lifted his shoulders like he was cold. He wore a nice sweater, but no jacket. "You forget. I convinced him to let you drive with me when I got my first car. And I convinced him to let me take you camping overnight for my sixteenth birthday. Both were a challenge."

"If I remember correctly, he threatened that you'd never walk normally again if you took advantage of me on that camping trip."

Jaden grinned. "Yes. But you can't take advantage of a willing participant. I knew I was safe."

"If he only knew what we did on that trip, he would have killed you."

Jaden chuckled. "It was sweet and romantic. We were kids exploring each other. And I think I wore three condoms just to make sure you didn't get pregnant, and he didn't cut my balls off."

Keri laughed too. "Funny that we were ever that innocent."

Her parents returned from their short drive, and when they got back, her father stood in front of Jaden. "It's an impressive car," he admitted. "But

I don't understand you. Why did you go through all this trouble? If it's to get close to Keri again, I'm telling you right now that I'll run you over with this car if you hurt her again."

"Sir, I'd want you to have this car even if Keri never spoke to me again. I'm not offering you the car to get close to her, but I won't lie; I'm happy that she's talking to me again, and I'd love to be her friend. We have a lot of history together, and I miss all of you."

Keri's throat tightened, and a lump formed, making it difficult for her to swallow. She could feel the sincerity in his words and saw how much he wanted to please her father. Hearing him say that he missed them—her entire family, not just her—touched her deeply.

Her father frowned, but he held out a hand. "Thank you, then. This is a generous gift, and I'm overwhelmed."

"I understand," Jaden said. "I can come over in a day or two and do the paperwork to transfer title if that's okay."

Her father nodded.

Keri jumped up and down and embraced her mother and her father. "I'm happy for you. Don't expect my gift to be this great, okay?" Although she knew he'd love his recliner.

"You've given me enough." Her father caressed the back of her head. "I know what it took to join forces with that knucklehead to do this for me."

Both Jaden and Keri laughed.

"Well, you two. Go on to the party. We're going to get inside where it's warm."

"Oh, I'm not going to the party," Jaden said.

"Why not? Keri, take him with you," her mother said.

"I'm sure he'd rather stand outside all night shoveling snow than go to a party full of kids."

Jaden shrugged. "I don't have anything else to do, but I don't want to butt into your night with your friends."

Keri rolled her eyes. He'd done nothing but push his way into her life. "They were your friends too, once upon a time." She grabbed a handful of his sweater. "Come on. If you don't go, I'll have no way of getting there. I'd have to borrow Dad's new car since I drove it here."

"True," he said.

They waved at her parents and got in his car.

"That went pretty well, except for the threat of killing me."

She laughed as she pulled on her seat belt. "That's only if you hurt me." She eyed him. "You're not planning to hurt me, are you?"

He started the car. "You're safe with me."

She gave him directions to the restaurant. "It's downtown. I'm warning you, it's a loud place with lots of kids and video games. If you'd rather drop me off and not go in, that's perfectly okay."

She'd prefer it if he didn't go with her, knowing that if he did, she would have to endure questions from her friends afterward.

He parked. "I don't mind. I might even play some video games. Remember all the Nintendo games we used to play at my uncle's house?"

"Ugh, yes. I thought inviting me over to play games was just an excuse to make-out, but, no, you really wanted to play games."

His deep laughter filled the car. "To be honest, my uncle would have killed me if he'd found us naked in my bedroom. It was okay if he messed around with women, but not me."

"Ah, that explains it. Okay then, let's get in there and join this party."

Jenn reserved a couple of tables in the back for parents to sit while the kids ran around dropping quarters into the games. Loud rock and roll music and video game sounds greeted them. It took a second for Keri's eyes to adjust to the darkness and flashing lights coming from all the machines.

"Keri," they called when they saw her. The moment they spotted Jaden, Keri could see the curiosity on their faces.

"Hey, everyone. You all remember Jaden."

Her friends exchanged glances before looking back at Jaden.

Jaden felt the scrutiny immediately. It had been a long time since he'd seen his old friends. Only a few of Jenn's guests were people he'd gone to school with. Others were spouses or friends Jenn had made after, probably from work, kid playgroups, or wherever people made friends these days. Jaden waved and shook hands with those close to him.

He and Keri took a seat and ordered beers. Jenn and her husband Paul bought pizza for everyone and encouraged them to eat, but he wasn't hungry, so he declined.

He leaned back, stretched his legs, and took in the energy in the room. Excited shouts and cheers combined with the music and electronic sounds as children and adults alike played their favorite video games. Laughter and friendly banter from the dining tables echoed throughout the space, adding to the lively atmosphere. This wasn't Jaden's usual scene, but he had to admit that he liked watching families have fun together, even if it was while staring at screens and tapping buttons furiously on a machine. Eventually, parents rounded up their kids and forced them to eat at least one slice of pizza before returning to their games.

Keri helped to pass out paper plates and made sure the kids had a place to sit, but since their parents were there, she mostly sat beside Jaden and watched her friends get their kids settled with what looked like longing.

Jaden reached across and eased some hair away from her beautiful face.

She gazed at him and waited, maybe for him to say something, but when he didn't speak, she said, "You're staring."

"Sorry. Just watching you with your friends' kids. You'll have your own kids soon, Keri."

She leaned into him. "I hope you're right."

"You will. And you'll be a great mom. Are you feeling better? About the procedure and all that?"

"I felt better after talking to you. Thank you for listening. I'm sure it was uncomfortable. I didn't mean to dump all that on you."

He placed a hand over one of hers and caressed her knuckles with his thumb. "I'm willing to listen anytime. I may not have anything intelligent to say to make you feel better." He grinned. "But I can listen."

"What you said was perfect."

For a moment, he lost his ability to form a coherent thought, lost in her open and appreciative gaze, wanting more than anything to make her look at him like that always. "Keri, I —."

"Well, isn't this cute," Sam popped up beside them. "Brings back so many memories. Most of them bad, if I'm being honest."

Jaden turned away, pulling his hand away from Keri, and took a big gulp from his beer mug. Plastering a smile on his face, he faced Keri's best friend. "How have you been, Samantha?"

"Working, raising kids, you know, being an adult."

A guy wrapped an arm around her shoulder. "How long are we staying at this thing?" He asked.

"I don't want to hear any complaints from you."

He held his hand up. "I'm just asking." He looked at Jaden. "I'm Patrick. Sam's husband."

Jaden shook his hand. "Jaden."

"You look like you're having as much fun as I am," Patrick said.

He probably looked like a trapped rat being stared down by an angry cat. Sam was definitely in her protect-her-friend mode. "What could be better than pizza, beer, and old friends?"

Samantha scoffed.

"Right," Patrick said. "Interested in a game of pool or a nice shooting game?"

"Ah, sure," Jaden said, gazing at Keri, trying to determine if she was okay with that. When she didn't give him a clue one way or the other about how she felt, he pushed himself out of his seat and left with Patrick.

When the guys were out of hearing range, Samantha said, "Looks like things are progressing well with you two."

Keri shook her head. "Nothing to progress to or from. So, what do you have planned this week?"

"The usual. Preparations for Christmas Eve. Finish Christmas shopping."

"Maybe I'll go with you. I need to buy all the kids their gifts still."

"We can go tomorrow if you want. There's another storm coming in on Tuesday, so tomorrow might be the best day to finish up."

"Okay, let's go in the morning before I drive up to the shop."

"Are people still shopping for art this close to Christmas?"

"I'm getting a steady flow of customers. Which is good because I'll be closed between Christmas and New Year. And then it will definitely be slow as everyone recovers from Christmas spending. Maybe I'll head out to Hawaii in January."

Sam groaned. "I want your life."

Keri chuckled. "No, you don't. It can be very lonely at night."

"Hello? Have you noticed that my husband spends half his life at the base?"

"Yeah, but I wasn't talking about a man. Not really. At least you have the twins."

Sam wrinkled her nose. "Yeah, they're pretty special, but I wish I had a husband who was around more. I get lonely, too. I can imagine it's worse for you. We need to find you a man."

"Oh no," Keri said. "Been there, done that. I will never go on one of your blind dates again."

"I'm hurt."

Keri rolled her eyes. "Let's go watch the guys play pool."

Samantha grabbed her beer. "So, is Jaden falling for you yet?"

"Of course," Keri said. "Can't you tell?"

"Actually, I can." Samantha didn't sound happy about that.

CHAPTER FOURTEEN

J aden didn't really know how to play pool. He might have played a couple of times in his whole life. He didn't have time to play games. The only games he played involved making major deals, and they were games he played well.

Patrick hit the 12-ball into a side pocket and turned to dunk the 10-ball but missed. Jaden lost the first game to Patrick and was about to lose the second, but maybe he had a chance now.

"So, Sam tells me you and Keri used to date back in high school."

"We did." Jaden sank the orange five-ball.

"How did you let that go, man?"

Jaden glanced at him, then slammed number 4. Amazingly, he missed the pocket he was aiming at, but it bounced off the wall and into the opposite pocket.

"Nice angle shot. So, did you come back for a second chance?"

Jaden leaned on his cue. "Why do you ask?"

"Just making conversation. She's Sam's best friend, you know?"

Leaning across the table, Jaden aimed at the 7. If he got that one in, all he had was the 3-ball to go. He hit it gently, and it rolled right into the pocket. Jaden grinned. "Whoo. So, do you fly airplanes?" When they were talking about cars, they were clicking. Talking about Keri was a bad idea.

"No, I do mechanical work. I moved from active duty to civilian work after I married Sam and got the chance. I wanted to stay close to her."

Nodding, Jaden got ready to shoot the cue ball, when he noticed Keri and Sam coming their way. He tried to focus, but he could tell the second he hit the ball that he'd miscalculated. He hit the 3-ball on the side and missed the pocket.

"Awe, too bad," Patrick said.

"You're winning!" Keri said.

"I think I just lost," he said as Patrick banked his ball into a corner pocket. He drove the successive three balls in easily, and Jaden wondered if he'd been taking it easy on him.

"Eight ball in the corner pocket," he said, pointing his cue stick. Then, with ease, he shot it in. "That's two games, Jaden."

"Yep." His gaze lingered on Keri, who looked irresistibly adorable. "You ladies going to play next?"

"I think Jenn is rounding the kids up. They're going to walk to the ice-skating rink next."

"You're kidding?" Patrick said. "Shit, we have to go stand in the cold?"

"I'll keep you warm," Sam said, slipping an arm around his waist.

"Yeah? Well, that has a nice ring to it." He kissed his wife.

"Ice skating, huh?" Jaden asked Keri.

"We can walk down for a little while, if you don't mind. We don't have to stay for long."

"I'm good. Maybe I'll go out there with the kids. I have few ribs that aren't cracked yet."

"I think you will stay off the ice," she said, pointing at his chest. "Let's go. We'll see you down there," Keri said to Sam and Patrick.

They stepped out and breathed in the crisp air, mingled with the aroma of cooked food from the row of restaurants. "Awe, silence," he said.

"I know. It was so loud in there, wasn't it?"

"Ridiculously loud."

They strolled toward the ice-skating rink. He had this urge to reach for her hand. Of course, he couldn't do that. "Patrick seems like a nice guy."

"Yep."

"He said you introduced him to Sam."

"He told you I dated him, huh?"

"Ah, no. What?"

Keri laughed. "I'm kidding, though I did meet him first, and we became friends. I invited him to dinner along with a bunch of other friends. Sam came with her then-boyfriend, and Patrick couldn't take his eyes off her."

"Why didn't *you* date him?"

"Ah, no. I knew immediately he wasn't for me. The whole macho military thing wasn't working. So, anyway, at the end of the night, I gave him Sam's number."

"And the rest is history?" Jaden asked.

"Yep, which made me very happy because they were both my friends and perfect for each other."

They got to the little rink, which was surrounded by shops beautifully decorated with Christmas lights. He and Keri stood beside the massive Christmas tree until the others slowly arrived. Keri bounced up and down on her toes, trying to get warm.

"Cold? Why don't I go get us some hot chocolate?"

"That sounds amazing."

"I'll be right back." He walked a couple of blocks down to a coffee shop. When he got there, he decided to get hot chocolate for all her friends and their husbands. The barista gave him carriers that carried six cups each. He took a dozen cups to the freezing parents, who were watching their little ones on the ice.

"Oh my God," Jenn said, "thank you so much, Jaden. You are a life-saver."

He handed one to Keri, grabbed one for himself, and then let the others take the cups that remained.

Everyone thanked him.

"That was thoughtful," Keri said, moving up next to him.

He rubbed her back, and they drank hot chocolate as they watched the kids have the time of their lives. Jaden watched Keri's flushed face, laughing and enjoying the night with her friends. Had she always been such a beautiful girl who was so easily happy? He thought of all the complicated women he'd dated. Rich, gorgeous women. Amazingly dressed. Women whose scents lured him in like nymphs lured sailors on the high seas. But none touched his heart the way Keri did so easily.

"I'm frozen," she said to Sam, dropping a kiss on her cheek. "I'm out of here. Ready, Jaden?"

"Whenever," he agreed. The temperature seemed to have dropped.

"Thanks for coming." Everyone said goodbye, hugging, shaking hands, and waving as they walked away.

They hurried back to the car, running the last few steps.

"Hurry. Turn the car on," she said.

He did and ran the heater on high. After it had warmed up enough, he put the car in gear and headed back to her place.

"I'm going to have to take poor Mochi out, damn it."

He pulled up to her apartment. "I'll take him out. You get inside."

"I can't do that to you; he's my dog."

"Will he go with me?"

"He'll go with anyone who is fool enough to take him out."

Jaden opened the car door. "Let's go then."

She ran after him. As soon as she opened her front door, Mochi acted like Keri had been gone a month. She laughed and pulled off her gloves.

"You are such a drama queen." Mochi jumped on her as she hooked the leash on his collar. "Are you sure about this?" she asked.

Jaden took the leash. "Around the block?"

She nodded.

"I'll be back."

Mochi didn't need any encouragement. Jaden snapped the leash, and Mochi ran out in front of him and down the stairs.

Keri watched them leave, grateful and feeling a warmth that had nothing to do with being in her apartment. She closed the door and went to her kitchen to start her tea kettle. Then turned the fireplace on.

What a night. Fun and magical in so many ways.

The tea kettle whistled. She pulled down two mugs from her cupboard and added tea bags to cups. As she finished, Jaden knocked on the door.

"He did his business, a lot of it." Jaden handed her the leash.

She took it and towel-dried Mochi. "Go lay in front of the fireplace, Mochi." She pointed, and Mochi ran to his bed and dropped into it.

"Come in. I made some tea," she said.

"I think I'm just going to go." He pointed behind him with his thumb.

She tried not to be disappointed. Reaching for his jacket, she pulled on it. "Come on. I promise not to throw myself at you like last time," she said. "Come get warm."

Taking a step inside and pulling off his hat, he reached for her, drawing her toward him. His face was so close she could see deep into his sexy brown eyes. "What if I want you to throw yourself at me?" he asked. "What if I want you to do exactly what you're doing?"

"What am I doing?"

He shook his head. "We're not kids. You know what you're doing."

Did she? No, she didn't. She had no idea what she was doing or why, but she leaned forward and touched her lips to his cold ones like she'd wanted to do all night when he put a great big bow on the Lexus, when he sat beside her at the restaurant and made her feel less alone, when he'd walked beside her to the skating rink. Then, when he'd sweetly brought hot chocolate for everyone and stood so close she could feel his breath above her head, she almost kissed him then.

She indulged now in his taste and melted into his body. He angled his head and deepened the kiss. Gently, he lifted his head. "Keri, you feel so good."

"So do you."

"But, we can't do this," he said.

"I know."

"Your dad will run me over with the Lexus."

Gazing into his eyes, she smiled. "I don't have to tell him."

"I'm leaving soon. You know that."

"Then why are you here, making me feel like something is happening between us?"

He kissed her forehead. "Because part of me wants something to happen, but another part just wants to fix the mess I made before. I'm not going to fix it by repeating history, am I?"

Stepping back, she agreed. "No, I guess not. Though . . . this time, you're being honest. I know you're leaving." She gazed at him, wanting to lead him into her bedroom.

"When I leave, I don't want you to hate me again."

"I'm always going to hate you. You broke our engagement and ruined my dream of happily ever after."

He tightened his lips and shook his head, regret unmistakable in the way he looked at her.

"But I might miss you too, Jaden."

He groaned and pulled her into a tight embrace. "I'll miss you." He caressed the back of her head and ran his hands down her spine. "I think I've always missed you."

Placing her hands on his chest, she eased away from him. "Go before I don't want you to go, and we have a real problem."

He nodded and stepped away.

Closing the door and leaning on it after he left, Keri was beginning to realize that it *was* too late. She already didn't want him to go.

CHAPTER FIFTEEN

Jaden spent Monday morning closing a deal on the sale of his Lamborghini. The bank executive's wife decided that she absolutely wanted to buy her husband a car for Christmas. It would require Jaden to fly back home, sign the paperwork, and transport the car to her residence in Malibu. One day max.

"You tell me the best day for you, and I'll be there," Jaden said. He'd make a hundred thousand on this deal, so he'd do whatever was necessary. Plus, there were two new cars he planned to buy in the new year, so he could use the cash flow.

"Wednesday? Not a problem. Let's meet at . . . say five? You have my address, but I'll text it to you."

He ended the call. "Yes!" Grabbing his laptop, he pulled up the Delta website and booked an early morning flight on Wednesday. Checking his watch, he noticed it was almost two. No wonder he was hungry.

While strolling into the kitchen and opening the fridge, he checked his other email messages.

"Are you playing with your phone or getting food?" Uncle Frank asked.

Jaden put his phone on the counter. "Sorry. Did you eat lunch?"

"Yeah, a couple of hours ago. I didn't want to interrupt you. Seemed like you were doing some fast talking there."

"It was a big deal I was trying to close. I need to fly to California on Wednesday, but I'll be back the next day."

Frank grabbed his coffee cup and filled it, pulling up a chair at the table. "I made some baked chicken and mashed potatoes. In that red dish there."

"Thanks."

"Yep. Your work seems stressful. What happens if you can't find a buyer for a car?"

"I always do, eventually. Right now, it's not so bad because I have enough in the bank to buy cars and hold them until they sell. When I first started out, it was rough. I *needed* to sell my inventory to buy more. Now that I'm well known, these rich people call me. It's a sweet business."

Jaden warmed his food in the microwave and sat down to eat. "Looks like you're a little low on food. Should we go get some groceries?"

Uncle Frank nodded. "I think so, especially since the next storm is supposed to hit tomorrow. It's expected to be a big one."

"Let me finish, and we'll go."

Uncle Frank stood. "I'll go change. You never know when you're going to run into a sexy woman."

Jaden laughed and joked. "Comb your hair and put on some cologne, too."

"You bet."

Uncle Frank always looked and smelled good. The man, even now, could be vain.

"You going out tonight?" Uncle Frank asked when he returned.

"No, I thought we'd hang out together."

"What if I get a date?"

Jaden wiped his mouth to hide a smirk. "Are you planning on having a woman over? Sarah maybe?"

"I might."

"I like Sarah," Jaden said.

"Me too."

"So, why don't you do something about it?"

"I've done plenty. Not that it's any of your business."

"Oh. I guess I mean something more permanent."

Uncle Frank laughed. "You're not suggesting I move in with her or get married at my age?"

"You're never too old."

"Yes, after a certain age, you are definitely too old. She likes her house and independence, and I like mine. Last thing I want is a woman telling me what to do in my own house."

Jaden could understand that. "Well, if you have a date, I'll hide out in my room. Okay?"

That seemed to satisfy him. He nodded but then added, "On second thought, it's Monday night football. Maybe we should get some wings and potato wedges and more beer, and I won't invite anyone over."

So much for focusing on salads and healthy eating. "Sounds good, Uncle Frank. But just today. The rest of the week, no carbs or alcohol, okay?" Jaden patted his shoulder as they walked out.

While at the grocery store, Uncle Frank seemed to struggle to keep his balance, so he held onto his cart.

Jaden put the groceries into the cart. "You sure you're feeling okay?" he asked.

"Ever since I fell and hit my head a couple of years ago, sometimes I'm a little shaky. Age. It sucks."

"You fell? You didn't tell me that."

They turned the corner of the snack aisle, and Frank tossed in a bag of sour cream and onion chips. "We haven't talked in the last few months.

Plus, I was fine. They got my blood pressure meds wrong. Then, after I hit my head, I started with these dizzy spells."

Jaden grabbed the bag of chips and put it back. "Did you tell the doctor?"

"Yes, I told the doctor. That's why he changed my medication. You're a pain in the ass, you know that? I wanted those chips."

"I meant that the dizzy spells are continuing." Jaden ignored his comment about the chips.

Uncle Frank headed to the checkout lane. "Not really. Doctors just make things worse."

"Uncle Frank, you need to tell the doctor. I'll go with you if you want. When I get back from L.A., okay? Make an appointment."

"I don't need you to go with me."

Jaden placed an arm around his uncle's back. "Of course you don't. But I still want to go, just to get on your nerves."

"Yeah, you're good at that."

Keri played Christmas music and wrapped the toys she bought for her friends' kids and for her niece and two nephews. Shopping with Sam had been fun. They'd gone to Walmart and Target to get most of the toys for the younger kids. Then, they visited a couple of specialty stores. Her nephew loved baseball caps, and her niece loved novelty earrings that looked like ice cream cones or fish or cookies.

Thankfully, the preoccupation with finding the perfect gifts took all their focus, and Sam didn't bring up Jaden or ask her why she had brought him to Jenn's party. But when they stopped to buy hotdogs in the mall food court, Sam said that Patrick liked him. "I had to tell him that you weren't really interested in Jaden but that it was all a game."

"You told Patrick?" Keri frowned.

They sat at a table with their orange trays that held their hotdogs, fries, and drinks. Sam shrugged. "Patrick said it was mean. But when I explained why, he kind of understood."

"Maybe you shouldn't have said anything. Jaden's a different person now, and so it doesn't seem necessary to get even."

"Then what are you doing with him?"

That was a good question. She didn't have an answer. "It started out with the idea of giving him a taste of his own medicine, and if he had been the jerk I expected him to be, I would have done it." Although humiliating Jaden had never sat well with her. She doubted she would have embarrassed him and herself in front of others, even if he had been a jerk. "But now, there's no need for me to go out with him anymore. He might be a commitment-phobe or a guy married to his work, but he's also a nice person. I have no intention of hurting him."

She'd expected Sam to tell her she was too soft, or a sucker, but she took a bite of her hotdog and nodded. "Sometimes letting things go and moving on is the best strategy. I'm sure by now he realizes what he's missed." She winked.

She wanted to share more, tell Sam about the kisses, and ask her what she thought it meant. But it was nothing. And she couldn't admit to having feelings for a guy who had left and forgotten about all their dreams and plans together.

After the shopping excursion, Keri rushed to work with a trunk full of toys and worked non-stop helping customers find last-minute gifts.

Finally, after her busy day, she sat in her quiet apartment wrapping presents. As she looked at the toy trucks and Lego sets, she wished she could have been wrapping the gifts for her own children. She placed a hand on her abdomen, wondering if she was creating a baby right now. What a miracle life was.

She sighed and went to make a cup of hot chocolate. If it was meant to be, it would happen. When the water got hot, she poured it into the cup and stirred. Taking it to the couch, she sat beside Mochi and thought of Jaden. What had he done today? What was he doing tonight? It was best to put him out of her mind, too. She wasn't sure when he was leaving. After Christmas, and then she'd probably never see him again. If she did, it would be periodically when he chose to visit his uncle.

She finished her hot chocolate, washed her cup, and then arranged the presents under her tree. "For now, Mochi, it's just you and me."

Mochi stretched and came to lick her face.

She rubbed the top of his head. "Let's go for a quick walk before bedtime. What do you say? You want a walk?"

Mochi barked and ran to the door.

CHAPTER SIXTEEN

Anticipating a snowstorm, Keri decided to arrive at work early on Tuesday, since she would need to close and drive home before it got dark and the snow got too heavy. She didn't expect to get many customers today anyhow, but a couple of artists were dropping off paintings and Christmas pottery, so she planned to meet with them this morning.

Snow started to fall while on her drive to Custer, a little earlier than expected. But the roads were clear, so she made it to her shop without a problem.

Debbie arrived with two beautiful new paintings: one of an elk peaking between snow-covered pine trees and another of Sylvan Lake at sunset. Purples and various shades of reds and oranges gave the scenery a warm, peaceful feel. Debbie's art was unique because she painted on metal sheets.

"That one's not very Christmasy or wintery, but I thought someone might like it, anyway."

"It's gorgeous! Plus, most of my Christmas items won't sell after this week, so I'm glad you're bringing me other items."

"I also made you some homemade peppermint fudge bars."

"No way! Really? Those look sooo good." Keri gave her a hug. "Thank you so much, Debbie."

"Have a Merry Christmas. Are you going to be open next week?"

"Probably not. It will be too close to Christmas. Hugs to your family."

After Debbie left, Keri got busy organizing products and entering items into inventory, including Debbie's two pieces. About a dozen customers stopped in before the snow got too thick. The shopping season was almost over, and everyone wanted to beat the weather.

A couple of hours later, her phone rang, and it was her second artist saying she wasn't going to stop by because the snow was just too heavy to travel. Keri looked up and out of the large window and couldn't believe the amount of snow that had fallen. There had to be four or five inches of snow already.

"No problem," Keri said. "Stay home and be safe. I may close and leave."

She walked outside to look at the road, but it hadn't been plowed. Checking the weather on her phone, she saw that it was only going to get worse. "Damn." She dialed her mother. "Mom, the snow is awful out here. It looks like I'm going to be stuck overnight."

"Oh no, I'm sorry, Honey. It's snowing here too, but not too heavy yet."

"You're going to have to keep Mochi with you. I didn't expect it to snow so much so early."

"That's okay, Keri. Don't worry about the dog; he's a good boy and no bother."

"Okay, I just wanted to let you know. Didn't want you to worry."

"You take care, stay warm, and I'll see you in the morning."

Keri sighed as she ended the call. She should have brought a good book. It was going to be a long, frosty night."

Jaden grabbed the envelope with the pink slip and sales paperwork to take to Mr. Anderson and slipped it into his jacket pocket.

"You should wait a few days until after the snowstorm," Uncle Frank suggested, as he gazed out of the living room window around the Christmas tree.

Jaden picked his keys off the coffee table. "I'm flying to California tomorrow, so I want to finish this deal and give my bookkeeper the paperwork to close the books before the end of the year." He'd need the loss on the books, especially with the sale of the Lamborghini. "I'll be back in a bit before it gets too bad out there."

He hurried outside and drove to the Anderson home. Keri's mom seemed surprised to see him when he knocked on her door.

"I should have called first. I'm sorry. Uncle Frank probably has your number. But I brought the paperwork that Mr. Anderson will need to register the car."

"Come inside, Sweetheart." She ushered him in and called her husband.

"Oh, Jaden," Mr. Anderson said. "What are you doing out in this weather?"

He handed him the envelope. "I wanted you to have this. I need to fly back to California on business tomorrow."

"Oh, you're not coming back."

"I am. But just in case, I didn't want to hold on to it. I've signed everything over to you, so you should be good to go." His car crash had made him a bit paranoid about leaving anything unfinished. What if his plane went down, and he never signed over the car? Look at what happened to his parents.

Mr. Anderson nodded. "Again, I can't thank you enough, Jaden. I drove the car around yesterday just to drive it. It's a fine vehicle, much nicer than anything I would have bought myself."

"I'm glad you like it."

"I'm going to get snow tires for it after the storm in a couple of days."

Mrs. Anderson placed two cups of coffee on the table. And she sat down across from them. "Have some hot coffee, Jaden."

"Thank you. Please tell Keri that I'll call her when I get back. I don't want her to think I'm taking off without saying goodbye again."

Mrs. Anderson smiled. "We sure will. I won't see her until tomorrow. She called to say she's going to stay at the store tonight; it's snowing too hard for her to make it home." She glanced at her husband. "So, we have the dog all night, Charles."

"Yeah, I thought she was being foolish driving to Custer this morning. But I'm glad she has enough sense to stay put. Keeping the dog is no problem. At least we have a yard for him to do his business."

"Uh, Keri's going to spend the night alone at her shop in Custer?" Jaden asked, not liking the sound of that at all.

Mr. Anderson sipped his coffee and nodded his head. "I guess so."

Jaden stood. "I'll drive out there to stay with her."

"Oh no," both Mr. and Mrs. Anderson said, looking more concerned about his decision than the fact that their daughter was going to be all alone in a snowstorm. "It's too dangerous for you to drive in this," Mr. Anderson said. "She's safe. You go home."

Jaden shook his head. "If I go now, I can get out there before the roads get too bad."

"You're crazy, Jaden." Mr. Anderson frowned. "If she chose to stay, it's because she can't get out. The roads will be closed."

"She probably doesn't even have any food or water."

Mrs. Anderson shook her head. "Keri took a lunch. She always does. And she has snacks there. And, of course, she has water. She has a little kitchen area in the back of the store. Honey, you're sweet to be concerned, but we wouldn't be so calm if we thought she was in danger."

"I'm going." He hurried to the door. "Thank you for everything, and I'll see you all when I get back from California." Jaden ran to his car. He drove through Safeway and picked up a couple of sandwiches, some chips, and water. He also saw they were selling Christmas throws as gifts, so he grabbed a couple. Then he got on the road to Custer. The main roads were being constantly plowed, so he drove slowly, climbing into the higher elevations without a problem.

As he got deeper into the hills on Highway 16, the snow fell heavier, and it became harder to see. Jaden had the wipers going at full speed and the air blowing on the windows to keep them from fogging, but it was still getting difficult to see the road. Plus, the plows either hadn't been by lately, or they weren't working at all.

Every once in a while, his tires would spin until they caught again. But he kept slowly making progress. Keri probably would have been fine, but he didn't like the idea of her being alone in this mess. What if she lost power to her store and had to be there until morning with no food or anything warm?

The snow got thicker and thicker, and the car slipped across the top of the snow. More than driving, he felt like he was skiing across the top of the snow. He fought for control, but the tires lost all traction, and he wasn't even sure he was still on the road. The visibility had also gone to about zero. His car started to slide sideways. "Shit," he said, fighting for control before he hit a snowbank and got stuck.

Thankfully, he was only traveling at about ten miles per hour and the landing in the snow was soft, which thankfully did not trigger the airbags. His ribs appreciated that. He got out and tried to clear enough snow from the front tires to move forward. But no matter how much snow he managed to push away from the tires, it wasn't enough. The car wouldn't budge. Then he kicked the snow from behind the back tires and shook the car. He tried to back up, but again, the tires spun, and the car slid deeper into the bank. "Great."

Jaden dusted the snow off his jacket and hat and called AAA to get roadside assistance. The guy who answered told him it would be a while, but someone would help him as soon as they could. About twenty minutes later, a snowplow went by. A guy stopped and asked if Jaden needed him to call someone.

"I called for help already."

"Okay, sit tight then. We're getting the roads plowed as much as possible, but with the snow coming down this hard, we're falling further and further behind. Still, the tow truck should be able to get through soon."

It took about an hour, but finally, a tow truck came and pulled him out of the snowbank. "Do you want me to take the car somewhere? If you try to drive in this, you're going to end up in another snowbank on the side of the road."

Jared gave him Keri's address. "Can you take me and the car there?"

"Yep, get in."

Jaden was freezing. His feet were soaked. His hands, even with gloves, were red and numb.

But the truck drove about twenty miles per hour and eventually reached Keri's shop, where it unhooked his car. Jared gave him his credit card and signed whatever was on the driver's iPad. He didn't know what it said and didn't care.

Keri opened the door to her shop. "What the heck. Jaden?"

He'd never been so glad to see a friendly face in his life, even if she looked at him like he was insane.

CHAPTER SEVENTEEN

J aden waved at the tow truck driver, then took the food and blankets
out of his car. "Get inside. I'll be right there."

But she held the door open for Jaden as drifts of snow danced around
her. She held her jacket tight around her body.

Jaden ran stiffly inside; he couldn't feel his toes anymore. Fighting
against the wind, Keri pulled the door closed and locked it. The sky was
almost dark already, though it was probably only about four in the afternoon. She gawked at him and shook her head. "Do you want to tell me
what you were thinking coming up here?"

"I will, but right now, I'm frozen. I need to take these shoes off."

"Come here." She pulled him to the back of the store where she had a
small office and a storage room. "Take those wet jeans and socks off."

His jaw chattered, but he did as she said. She switched on an electric heater and placed his clothes beside it to dry. Then she handed him a pair of Christmas pajama bottoms.

"What's this?"

"What does it look like? Not exactly art, but I order a few sets for customers who like to buy extra gifts along with their artwork." She dried his feet and reached for another item. "I don't know if these Christmas slippers will fit you, but you can try them on."

Stepping into the blue pajama bottoms with little white snowmen, he felt ridiculous, but they were flannel and warm, so he'd wear the embarrassing clothes. He slipped on the manly red slippers with white snowflakes and the words Ho Ho Ho all over. Then she handed him a blanket. "Wrap this around your legs, too, until you get warmer."

"I'm fine. This is enough. Thank you."

She sat beside him on a stool. "Now. What are you doing here? Have you lost your mind?"

He smirked. "I came to save you from being alone and helpless in the snow." He looked down at his legs. "But I guess you saved me."

"You are seriously crazy."

"I pictured you alone, with no power, no food, no warm blankets. I even bought a couple of throw blankets at Safeway." He stopped talking to gaze at her, a woman who was in complete control and had managed without him for the last ten years. "But I guess you were doing okay without me."

She shook her head in disbelief, her lips parted as if she didn't know what to say, but slowly they lifted into a smile. "I could use the company. It can get creepy here at night, especially when the wind blows and the glass windows rattle."

"I brought sandwiches," he said.

"That sounds wonderful. I ate my bowl of chili that I brought for lunch a few hours ago."

Frowning, he wondered what had really possessed him to go out in this weather. He just had to know that she'd be okay. He never would have been able to sleep knowing she was here alone. "I was worried about you."

"I can see that. You didn't have to be. But thank you."

He nodded.

"Did you get stuck in the snow? Is that why the tow truck pulled you in?"

"Yeah, I slid into a snowbank. It's bad out there, but thankfully, my rental car is okay."

"Thankfully, *you're* okay," she said. "Should we eat?"

"Yeah," he stood and went back into the front of her store. He grabbed the Safeway bags and pulled out the sandwiches and chips. "I have water bottles too, but I left them in the car."

"I have water," she said. "Or, better yet," she pulled a bottle of wine from one of her horseshoe wine racks. "It's a prop, but it's real. You want wine?"

"Why not?"

She went to the storeroom and came back with a couple of coffee mugs. "Not classy, but they will work. I don't have a corkscrew, but maybe we can push the cork through."

"Sure." He grabbed the blankets and stretched them out on the floor. "A picnic in an art store. Not many people can say they've done that, huh?"

"I love it." She crossed her legs and sat on the thin flannel blanket while Jaden pushed the cork into the bottle with a knife she gave him. When it went in, she clapped her hands.

He poured rich Merlot into the coffee mugs. "You have good taste in props."

"Mmm," she moaned and raised the cup to her lips. "Oh, wait, should I drink this since I'm trying to get pregnant?"

"Do you know if the procedure worked?"

"Not yet. It's too early."

Jaden shrugged. He didn't know anything about pregnancies. "I say go for it. Even if it worked, I'm sure it's safe."

Keri shrugged. "I'm going to enjoy this. Cheers," she held up her cup. He touched his cup to hers. They unwrapped their sandwiches and ate. "This is really good. Thank you, Jaden."

"My pleasure."

"I mean, really, thank you. You risked your life to come here. It was stupid, but really sweet."

He chuckled, feeling self-conscious, which was strange because he usually loved when women praised him for doing things for them. He was also used to buying women expensive things, taking them out for a quality meal, and paying for expensive vacations. In comparison, what had he really done for Keri? "It was worth it, just so I could sit here having a romantic meal with you in blue Christmas pajama bottoms and red slippers."

Keri laughed. "You do look super sexy."

He enjoyed making her laugh. As he looked out, the snow kept falling, slowly accumulating and transforming the parking lot into a white blanket, isolating them from the rest of the world. "You think it's going to stop by morning? I have a plane to catch."

"Are you serious? It's going to snow all night. A plane where?"

"I'm supposed to meet a client tomorrow in L.A. She's the wife of this bigshot executive, and she's buying him a Lamborghini for Christmas. She's been debating it for weeks, and she finally decided to go for it the other night. I'm flying out tomorrow, then coming back the next day."

Keri ate her sour cream and chives Lays chips and checked the weather on her phone. "I hate to say this, but unless your flight is in the evening, I don't think you're going to make it. We're easily going to get about sixteen inches of snow." She showed him her phone.

"Great. I have an early morning flight." Jaden took out his own phone. "Excuse me a sec." He dialed his client's number, pacing at the front of the store. "Hey Bethany, Jaden. Yeah, yeah, I'm looking forward to it too, but I have a small glitch . . . no, nothing is wrong with the car. I'm stuck in a fucking snowstorm. I know, can you believe it?" He listened to her talk about how inconvenient lousy weather could be, but then she started to freak out about not having the car in time for Christmas.

"Listen, you will have the car in time. Can we meet on Friday instead? This will give me two days to get out of here . . . you're flying to Mexico on Friday?" Shit, shit, shit. He kept pacing, running a hand through his hair. "Thursday, then. For sure, I'll be stuck here tomorrow morning, but I can fly out at night or early Thursday morning."

His solution was not ideal for her. She complained that she needed to get her hair done and would be super busy on Thursday. "I counted on you to keep your word for Wednesday, Jaden," she said, sounding less like the friendly and cute socialite she'd been until now and more like a stern schoolteacher.

"I know. I'm really sorry. If I could drive twenty hours to get to you tomorrow, I would. What if I cut a couple of thousand off the price of the car for your trouble?"

At that, her tone changed, and she agreed. Jaden snapped his fingers and smiled. "Perfect. Then Thursday it is. I'll see you at five? Three, ah . . . okay. I'll tell the airline to get me there at three or else. You have a good night."

He hung up and breathed a sigh of relief.

Keri watched him. "Unbelievable. Are all the people you deal with like that?"

Jaden dropped back onto the blanket. "They're spoiled and used to getting what they want when they want it, if that's what you mean."

"You just lost two thousand dollars because you're stuck in the snow. How is the weather your fault? She wasn't very understanding."

He took a drink of wine and poured more into both their cups. "A drop in the bucket. I'll easily make eighty to a hundred thousand on this deal. If I have to fly back without sleeping, I'll do it. If I have to kiss her ass, I'll do it. What time do you think we'll get out of here tomorrow?"

"It really depends on the roads and how long it snows. If it stops tonight, we have a good chance of getting out by noon. If it keeps snowing in the morning, it will be later."

"Hmm, give me another second."

"Do what you need to do." She stood. "I'll clean up here."

"Leave the wine."

"Of course." She winked, and damn, for a second, he forgot what he was going to do.

He sighed and called Eduardo. "Hey pal, I might need you for a few hours on Thursday."

"Didn't you say we were done for the year?" Eduardo asked.

"Yeah, but Bethany decided on the Lamborghini at the last minute." He watched as Keri came back with the blanket she'd given him in the storeroom. She wrapped a couple of Christmas pillows she had on display with our jackets to protect them and spread out the blanket.

"That's awesome!" Eduardo's voice drew him back to the conversation.

"I know, and I was planning to fly back tomorrow morning, but I'm stuck in the middle of nowhere under a mountain of snow. They will probably clear the roads tomorrow morning, and somehow, I'll have to dig my car out and make a path to the road. Anyhow, I won't be able to fly out until tomorrow night or early Thursday morning. If anything happens and I can't leave, I'll need you to be there to do the paperwork and have her car delivered where she needs it to go."

"My wife is going to be pissed, but I'll work it out."

"Thank you. Tell her I will send her to her favorite spa to enjoy a day of pampering. Whatever she wants."

"Dude, you know a way to a woman's heart. She'll love that."

"Thanks. I'll let you know if I need you. If I get out of here in time, I'll take care of Bethany myself, but I'll probably still need to get picked up at the airport."

Jaden ended the call and dialed the airline. "Making our beds?" He asked Keri while he waited for his call to connect.

"We might as well go to sleep early. There's nothing else to do."

He was on hold.

"Did you place us six feet apart for a reason? Are you sick, or are you afraid you'll be tempted by these pajama bottoms after all?" He gave her a macho pose.

She laughed. "I roll around a lot." But she moved them a couple of inches closer together.

An airline representative came on the line, so he explained his dilemma. She took a few minutes but was able to get him an early morning Thursday flight. He'd get into L.A. by one in the afternoon. It helped that California was an hour earlier.

"You are wonderful. Hey, can I get an additional ticket?"

"Let me check," said the representative.

"Keri, come with me to L.A."

She looked up. "What? I can't leave. I have Mochi, and—."

"And what? You're going to close the store down anyway, right? It will just be for a day or two. Your mom can keep the dog."

She frowned and chewed on her lower lip.

"Don't overthink it. It will be fun. I want to show you my cars. Come on."

The representative came back and said she had two first-class seats available. He held out his hand and whispered. "What do you say? Live a little. Say yes."

"Ah . . . okay, I guess."

"Awesome," he said. "I'll take the additional ticket."

Now, his spirits soared. After a stressful couple of hours, he relaxed. He tossed his phone on the blanket and dropped down beside her, taking her hand. "I can't wait to show you my place."

"I can't believe I'm doing this."

"Why not? Shit, I've decided at the last minute to fly to London, Germany, or to visit a woman I haven't seen in ten years, all on the spur of the moment."

Keri let go of his hand, pulled her knees up to her chest, and hugged her legs. "I'm not like that. Plus, didn't you say you came back to see your uncle?"

He stared at her. Suddenly, she looked vulnerable, shutting him out and curling into a small cocoon. "Maybe somewhere deep inside, I hoped I'd run into you. I didn't expect it to be my first night here, but who am I to complain about divine intervention?"

"Is that what it was?"

"Whatever it was, I'm grateful."

She nodded. "Me too."

They gazed at each other. He wasn't sure what this meant or where it left them, but he didn't want to analyze it. Being with Keri felt good, and he didn't want it to end. He didn't want to be apart from her now that they'd reconnected. She agreed to come with him to California. That was all that mattered.

CHAPTER EIGHTEEN

Keri couldn't look away from his ardent stare. At any second, he might bridge the gap between them and pull her arms away from the body. And if he did, she might not stop him. She was such a fool. Instead of having him fall for her, she was falling for him all over again. What a joke she was. But he was bigger than life, consumed her attention, no, demanded her attention. Not even a snowstorm kept him away. She wasn't strong enough to resist this kind of all-consuming attention. In so many ways, he filled the need she had to be wanted — a need he created when he left her.

Her phone rang, and they both jumped. Keri crawled to reach for the cell and saw that it was her mother. "Mom, hi." She cleared her throat, which had suddenly thickened. "I'm fine. Yes, Jaden made it. Barely. His car got stuck in the snow, but a tow truck pulled him in." She laughed at her mother's shock. Keri agreed that Jaden was nuts and told her not to worry. They were both fine.

"She says you're crazy," Keri said.

"I've been called worse things than that."

"Hey, I have dessert!" She went to the counter and got the fudge treat her client brought that morning. "Let's have some," she said.

Jaden's eyes widened. "Wow, that will give us a nice sugar rush."

"I know, right?" She cut a big piece for both of them, and they indulged. "Oh my God," she said as the chewy chocolate melted in her mouth. "I love my artists."

Jaden nodded as he chewed. "Incredible."

"My clients may not make me thousands of dollars, but this dessert is worth a million bucks," Keri said.

"You're really enjoying that, huh?"

"I may eat it all. Don't let me."

He laughed. "So, after we finish with Bethany on Thursday, I'll take you on a ride in one of my luxury cars. I'll let you choose which one you want to ride in."

"Okay, I'd love that. But I'm curious. Do you think spending so much money on a vehicle is indulgent?"

"Of course it is. But so what? So is buying useless art. No offense."

"I guess you're right." She leaned back on her pillow, completely satisfied. "But I don't buy it for myself. I enjoy working here, where I'm surrounded by other people's creativity. I don't need to collect art for myself."

"Maybe if you didn't sell art, you would buy it for yourself."

"Maybe." She looked around, loving her store and the people who helped her fill it.

He leaned back on his pillow, too, and scooted next to her. "The way I feel about it is that if other people get to buy the amazing cars I sell, I want to own a few of my own. It was years before I could afford to do it."

She lay on her side so she could look at him, and he did the same. "I never knew you had this desire to be wealthy. You never talked about it as a teen."

"My desire was to be successful, to feel wanted, and now that I have cars that important people want, it . . . I don't know."

"Fills a void or a need you had, maybe?"

"Yeah maybe. I'm the cool dude with the hot cars. Makes me feel important. Stupid, huh?"

Keri felt a tug in her heart for the man who worked so hard to create an image he found acceptable. "Wanting to be important or needed is not stupid. Plus, we all have those needs."

"Do you?"

She thought about it. "Maybe not to be important. But to matter to someone. I've had my parents who have always made me feel that I mattered and that I'm important to them. But I also have a desire to be needed. Maybe this is why I want to have kids."

He rolled on his back and placed his hands behind his head.

"You lost your parents when you were so young, Jaden. You didn't have anyone to remind you that you mattered except your uncle, who wasn't very nurturing."

Jaden chuckled. "No, he wasn't that."

"I'll turn the lights off so we can sleep. I'll keep the outside lights on, though, unless they'll bother you."

"They won't bother me."

She flipped the lights off and looked outside. "It's really coming down. I think we're going to be here half of tomorrow."

"I don't mind," he said.

"Are you cold? I can bring the electric heater that's in the storage room back here. I turned it off. Your jeans were almost dry."

"I'm fine."

For some reason, she didn't want to get back on her blanket beside him. She put the dessert in the storeroom, got a couple of waters out of her small fridge, and brought them to the front.

Finally, having nothing else to do, she got back on her blanket. She'd used the two blankets he brought to cover the floor, but she only had one to drape over them. "We can share, I guess."

"I don't need it right now."

She lay back. It felt strange to sleep beside him.

"I'd forgotten how quiet snowfall can be," he said, staring up at the ceiling. "It's kind of cool laying here surrounded by all your Christmas decorations while it's snowing outside."

The experience truly had a touch of magic to it. "It's like camping in a museum."

He was quiet for a while, and she thought he'd fallen asleep. "Keri?"

"Hmm?

"I have to pee."

She smiled. "Bathroom is in the back on the right."

He left, and she closed her eyes, unsure that she'd be able to sleep, but she had to try.

"It's big back there," he said when he returned. "You have a work area. What do you use it for?"

She sat up. "That's where I make my horseshoe wine racks."

"*You* make those?"

"I do."

He sat back cross-legged and slid closer so that their knees were almost touching. His blanket was right beside hers now. "You didn't tell me I bought one of your creations."

"You didn't ask who the artist was."

"That's super cool. You should brag a little more."

She shrugged. "I do it for fun. I'm not really very creative."

"Hell, I couldn't make something like that."

She sighed. "I'm not tired. It's going to be hard to sleep tonight, isn't it?"

"Well, it's early. At least it is for me; I don't usually go to sleep until much later, especially when I'm home."

"What do you usually do in the evenings when you're in California?"

"I work all the time, travel, socialize with clients, or network. When I'm home, I watch TV, exercise in my gym, and crash around two in the morning."

She shook her head. "We lead such radically different lives, Jaden."

"I guess so." He reached for a water bottle and took a drink, then rested his hands on his thighs.

"We must seem so boring to you."

"Who is we?" He grinned and pointed at her nose. "I don't think you're boring."

"I mean our lifestyle here."

"Different isn't boring. People are real out here. They work, raise their families, and eat home-cooked meals. That has its own appeal."

"Do you think you'd ever want that?"

He looked up as if considering it, then gazed back at her. "Sure. I mean, I don't want to end up like Uncle Frank."

"You think he's lonely?"

Jaden nodded. "Sometimes. He keeps busy. Still has girlfriends." He chuckled. "Sarah is his favorite."

She reached across, placing a hand on his knee. "You should spend more time with him, Jade. See him more often."

"I call him. We talk."

"You think that's the same?"

"Probably not." He covered her hand with his, absently caressing her fingers. "I plan to come back more often. I'm a flawed human being, Keri. But like you were saying, Uncle Frank wasn't all that affectionate, you know? I raised myself in many ways, so I'm used to being on my own. But he stepped up when I needed him. His life wasn't set up for a kid, and yet, he still took me in. I owe him."

Her hand clasped tightly around his, halting the gentle stroking. "You don't owe him. You should come back to see him because you love him."

Lifting his eyes, he nodded slowly. "Do you want me to come back more often?"

She leaned back, releasing his hand. "I am not involved in any way with you or your uncle. But I think he's getting older and might need you more."

Reaching for her chin, he forced her to look at him. "I meant so we could spend time together. Maybe recapture what we lost?"

The warmth of his hand sent a quiver down her spine, and she turned away. "We didn't lose anything, Jaden. You gave it up."

"What if I want to get it back?"

She shook her head, not liking the direction of this conversation.

Now, he reached for her, his hands tenderly encircling her upper arms. "Listen to me for a second. Is it that crazy? You're not with anyone. I'm not, either. Why can't we see each other? Hang out? Have some fun? See where it leads?"

It would lead to her getting hurt, just like last time. "Because we have completely different lives. We were just talking about that. Long-distance relationships don't work. Plus, I don't trust you."

His hands moved up and down her arms. "Oh Keri. You can trust me. But I do agree that it would be tough to have a relationship with my lifestyle." He released her. "And you deserve to have a man who will be here for you all the time, not just sometimes."

A lump formed in her throat. She didn't know what she deserved, but she did know she hadn't found anyone who interested her in ten years. And she wasn't likely to anytime soon. Jaden was here now, asking her to let go and have fun. Would that be so bad?

"You're right about my uncle. I plan to visit more often. You might get tired of seeing me." He dropped back down on his blanket.

The tension eased, and a gentle smile tugged at her lips as she watched him stretch out beside her like a holiday gift. "I'll let you know if I do." Following his lead, she lay back down on her side.

He turned to his side, facing her, and then reached across to ease whisps of hair off her face. "It's selfish, I know, but I just want to be part of your life again. Being with you feels like home."

"You can't go back, Jaden," she whispered. "But this will always be your home. Even without me."

He slid his fingers down her face, gently caressing her cheek. "But I don't want it to be without you. You were my best friend."

"And you were mine. That's why it hurt so much to lose you."

His thumb traced her lips. "Life changed. You were a college girl, going places. I was headed nowhere and saw myself losing my best friend and my first love."

She shook her head and gripped his hand to stop his touch. What was he talking about? All she dreamed about was being with him. "Jade," she said, her heart breaking. "The only way you were ever going to lose me was by leaving me."

"I fucked up," he said, sounding choked up. He slid his thumb over the veins on the top of her hand, meeting her stare with so much want in his eyes that it took her breath away.

As if drawn by his hot gaze, she scooted forward and kissed him, sliding her lips softly against his.

He pulled back, blinked, looked down at her lips, and swallowed.

"Yeah, you did," she said. "You really fucked up. But here we are again. And for some reason, I still seem to want you."

He drew in a deep breath. "Yeah?" he whispered.

"And I hate myself for even admitting that."

"Why? I'm kind of irresistible. It's not your fault."

His joke made her laugh and broke the serious moment. "So, are we going to pretend we don't want to . . . be together?" she asked.

"I didn't say I wanted *you*," he said, his tone still playful.

She took his hand and placed it over her heart above her right breast, and she did the same with her hand on his chest. His heart thumped loudly. "Do you?"

All humor faded from his features, and he rolled onto his back. "I want you," he said, his voice rough with emotion. "I've never stopped wanting you. I realized that the second I saw you again."

She inched still closer to him, her body touching the side of his. She placed a hand on his belly, noticing the very obvious evidence of his arousal pushing up the flimsy pajama bottoms and feeling the raw desire between them. She didn't have the right or permission to reach down and touch him, but damn, she wanted to. "Well, then, here I am. What's stopping you?"

Jaden lifted his upper body, propping himself up on his elbows, his gaze softened. "I know I hurt you," he said. "And I hate myself for it. I don't want to do that again." He sat all the way up and wove fingers through her hair. "What's stopping me? Easy, I don't think you know what you want. On the one hand, you're telling me we can't go back, and we can't begin again, and on the other, you're telling me you want me. Which is it?"

She lifted her chin, understanding his confusion. But she was not confused. "I want you for tonight," she clarified. "I don't want an ongoing relationship with you."

"You're not a casual sex kind of girl."

"How do you know what kind of girl I am now?"

"Maybe I don't," he said, his hand sliding down and cupping her neck. "So, tell me. Be honest."

Sexual frustration made her close her hand into a fist and grip a handful of his shirt. "I'm not into casual sex normally," she admitted. "But maybe I need to have you touch me. To have you make love to me one more time."

Jaden took a deep breath. "I want to touch every part of you. But I can't promise it's going to be just once."

"Then touch me." She leaned over him until he eased onto his back, and she kissed him again. He hungrily returned the kiss, holding the back of her head with one hand and wrapping an arm around her waist with the other. His lovely erection pulsed between them, and she moaned. She was crazy to do this, but she wanted to indulge in these feelings. For once, she didn't want to just feel and not think. She lifted her head. "I don't need it to be more than sex. Okay?"

His hand slid to cup her bottom and pulled it against his hard penis. He stretched his head back, closed his eyes, and groaned. "Oh, Keri."

He lifted his hips, rubbing his hardness against her, ten-xing her desire.

Opening his eyes, he asked, "Are you sure about this?"

"I'm on top of you. I'm pretty sure." Then she added. "I know what I want." She cupped his face with both her hands and kissed him to show him that she very much wanted him.

He reached up and pulled her top off, gazing at her bra-covered breasts. "Oh man, gorgeous." He released her bra hooks, freeing her breasts. He took one of her nipples in his mouth and sent a rush of pleasure down her body. Both his hands were on her bottom now, pulling her against him, teasing her with what was waiting for her inside his boxer shorts.

The heat was almost too much for her. "Mmm Jaden," she moaned. "Take your clothes off."

He rolled her onto her back and pulled off his t-shirt. She reached to run her fingers down his chest, noticing his yellowing bruises. "Does it still hurt?"

"Not as much. Right now, my dick aches more."

She smiled. "I can help you with that." Finally, she did what she'd been dying to do, and she touched him through the clothes, and he inhaled sharply. Slowly, she slipped her hands through the elastic of his pajama bottoms and into his boxer shorts, reaching for his pulsing, velvety penis. As she slid her hand up and down, her thumb circling the edge of his swollen top, his arms trembled. "You're killing me," he said. "But don't stop."

She chuckled. "I'm not planning to. At least not yet." She kissed his chest and nipped at his nipples.

"Oh fuck," he said and jumped away from her. "That's it. Take your jeans off."

"I want you to take them off."

"Gladly." He reached for her waistband, his hands shaking, and slowly slid them down her legs.

"Jaden?"

"What?"

"What are you thinking?"

"Seriously?"

"Yes."

He turned passion-filled eyes to her face, then down her body. "That you're beautiful." He leaned down and kissed her. "That I must be dreaming, though in my wildest dreams, I never thought I'd get to make love to you again. What are you thinking?"

"Trying to remember the last time we were together like this."

He stared at her, a hard, dark stare. Without a word, he ran both thumbs over her puckered nipples, increasing her need; then his fingers trailed down her ribs and stomach, almost burning her already flushed skin. "Stop. Don't think. Just feel." His fingers slid further down, into her panties where they slid into her wet folds, caressing and making her shudder. "Just feel, Keri. That's right." His fingers slipped deeper inside her.

She closed her eyes and felt every delicious stroke, felt his mouth come down on her left nipple, then her right. She felt her heart beat erratically. Then she opened her eyes and gripped his head, pulling it up to gaze into his eyes.

"How does it feel?" he asked.

"Like I need you to be inside me."

He kissed her and slid his fingers out off her, making her want to protest, but he stood and took off those silly pajama bottoms and his boxers. He looked strong and hard and gorgeous. Oh, yes, she wanted all of him.

Then he bent down, touching the heat on the other side of the silky fabric of her panties with his lips, driving her to the brink of madness. Bending down lower, he ran his tongue on the outside of her already wet panties. "What do you feel now?" he asked, gazing up at her.

"Hot. Frustrated."

He slid her panties all the way down her legs. "You're definitely hot. What are you thinking?"

"Oh, Jaden, please stop talking."

Chuckling, he stretched over her, easing her legs apart with a knee. "Ah . . . shit, I don't have a condom."

"You don't carry one with you for all your liaisons?" she joked.

"I don't have one," he repeated. He dropped his forehead on her shoulder. "Oh Keri, tell me you don't want me to stop. I can't. I need to be inside you, to feel you tremble in my arms when you come."

God help her; she didn't want him to stop either. But if they didn't, they both knew what they were risking. "Then make love to me."

He kissed the side of her neck. "I won't leave you again." He whispered. "No matter what."

She grabbed ahold of his head and pulled it up. "I don't care if you do."

"Keri —."

"I don't need empty promises." She was prepared to raise a child by herself, no matter how it happened.

"Oh, Keri. You stupid girl, I'm falling in love with you again, can't you see that?"

Why did he have to say that? She pulled his head down and kissed him, wrapping her legs around his hips, hugging his body against hers, as he plunged into her repeatedly, sending her into the kind of ecstasy she hadn't experienced, maybe ever. As he ended with a final thrust and cry, her body convulsed with a released desire that left her weak. She swore that the Christmas lights in her store became brighter. For a minute or two, she held on tightly to him, pretending he was hers like he'd been the first time they'd made love.

But he lifted his head and kissed her softly. "I was a little rough."

"You were marvelous."

He grinned. "Tell me more."

She laughed and caressed his back. "I don't have showers here, but we can clean up in the bathroom."

"I'm not ready to clean up," he said. "I want to repeat that a couple more times tonight."

"Mm," she said. "I think I'm finally ready for sleep. Grab the bigger blanket and hold me."

But he stood and brought back some wet paper towels to wipe each other clean, before slipping in beside her and pulling her back against his chest. "Good night."

"Night, Jaden."

"Hey, before you go to sleep," he whispered. "I want to tell you that this is the best night I've had in about ten years. Being with you was incredible. I feel like I'm in heaven."

She opened her eyes and gazed at him over her shoulder. "You're going to break my heart with talk like that, you stupid boy."

"I promise I won't." He dropped little kisses on the back of her shoulder. "I will never break your heart again."

Then why did her heart race when she gazed at him, so afraid of what she felt inside? But she admitted, "This is the best night I've had in ten years, too."

He kissed the side of her face, and she closed her eyes, enjoying the feeling of being encased in the arms and legs of the only man she'd ever loved and probably ever would.

CHAPTER NINETEEN

Keri awoke with a start, pushing Jaden's arm off her. Her muscles ached from sleeping on the hard floor.

"What's wrong?" Jaden asked, his voice deep and thick as he struggled to wake up.

She rested her elbows on her knees and ran her hands through her hair. "Ugh, my head. My back. Everything is sore. And oh my God, my customers could look through the window and see us lying here naked."

"Whoa, slow down. There's a million feet of snow out there. No one is coming." He reached across and rubbed her shoulder. "Come here."

"No, Jaden. Don't."

He kissed her shoulder. "Let me hold you."

His tone was so sweet that she leaned against him, and he wrapped his arms around her waist.

"Just enjoy these last few hours of being locked away from the world," he said.

"You're going to have to find your car and blow the snow off if you hope to get home tonight and to the airport tomorrow morning."

"Later." His lips sweetly stroked her neck. A shiver ran down her spine as his lips traced a path of desire along her neck, sending waves of pleasure through her body.

"I'm not sleeping with you again." Her breathy words didn't sound convincing even to her.

His hands moved to her breasts, which were already puckering. His breath deepened, and he gently nipped at her earlobe. Then one of his hands slid down her belly and settled between her legs, a finger slipping inside her wet, swollen body. Her head dropped back onto his shoulder as he stroked her.

Now, her breath was becoming uneven. "Stop, Jaden" she pleaded.

"Why?"

"Because I'm . . . I just woke up . . . and I'm overly sensitive right now."

"What do you mean?" He bit her neck playfully. "What will happen if I keep touching you like this?"

She pushed his hand away and turned around, straddling him and wrapping her arms around his shoulders, her fingers buried in his hair. "Put yourself inside me."

He didn't argue, and within seconds, his hard penis was pushing up into her, filling and stretching her body. She gasped. "Oh you feel so good." She moved up and down the length of him as his hands squeezed her bottom. "Jaden," she cried.

"You're so beautiful, so hot," he said. He reached between them, finding her clit and sliding his thumb over it, then pinching it between his first and second fingers.

It was like an electric shock going through the core of her body; her body convulsed violently, and she collapsed against him. Jaden followed, his hot semen shooting into her and his arms crushing her against him.

She held him, tears filling her eyes. This felt so good, so right, the feelings were so intense, and it was about to end.

"Damn, that was spectacular," he said. "Now, that's the way to wake up."

She eased back and looked at the satisfied smirk on his face. "Didn't I tell you I wasn't sleeping with you again?"

His hands came to her face, and he pulled her down for a loving kiss. "When did you turn into such a liar?"

Pushing his shoulders, she stood unsteadily. "You're too much of a temptation."

"Mm," he said, leering at her. "So are you."

"I'm going to get dressed and make coffee."

"You have coffee? God, I love you."

She stopped dead and frowned.

"Ah, I mean. You know, figure of speech."

She nodded and went to the bathroom to clean up. Her legs were shaking as she sat on the toilet, and her heart thumped hard inside her chest. She wasn't sure if she was frightened or ecstatic. Maybe both. *Don't get emotionally attached. Just enjoy it.* And she had. It was mind-blowing sex, and that's all it had to be. She stood and washed her face. She gave herself a towel bath and got dressed. Then she went out to make coffee.

Jaden slipped his boxer shorts on and gazed outside at the unbelievable amount of snow. Somehow, he had to get out of here today, but it didn't look promising. Keri stepped up beside him and handed him a cup of coffee. She looked refreshed, with her hair up on her head, fully dressed, with no trace of the exciting woman he'd held all night. "Thanks," he said.

"Have you seen a snowplow pass by?"

The street was quite a few yards away. To get to her store, you had to enter a long driveway. "Not yet. Thanks for the coffee, but I'm freezing. I'm going to go get dressed."

"Go ahead. I'm going to do a little work if you don't mind."

He dropped a kiss on her lips and headed to the back to clean up and dress. Thankfully, his jeans were dry, not that they would stay that way once he went out to shovel her long-ass driveway. Snow had buried his car, too.

When he returned, she was on her computer. She'd picked up the blankets, and her store was back to looking like it had when he'd arrived yesterday. He sat to enjoy his coffee and called Eduardo to tell him he'd be able to meet with his client after all, but he needed him to take care of a few things. He gave him all the instructions.

"Does this mean my wife doesn't get her massage? She was looking forward to it much more than having me at home."

Jaden laughed. "Actually, I'd already planned to get her that for Christmas."

"Ah, pretty sneaky."

"Do me a favor and get the paperwork ready. The DMV stuff and all that; it will speed up the sale. Also, load the car onto the flatbed tow truck so we can transport it to her house."

"You got it. Have a safe trip home."

"Yep."

Jaden watched Keri work. He strolled to the counter, leaning across it. "You have become such a beautiful woman, do you know that?"

Keri smiled. "Thank you."

"I can't believe some guy hasn't snatched you up."

She stopped typing and sat back on her stool. "Relationships are complicated. That's what I've come to realize after so many years. There's a lot of compromising. And the older you get, the less you feel like changing to make others happy."

He'd never thought of it that way. "Why should you have to change?"

"Someone always has to, even if it's as simple as when you eat dinner, how you fold your towels, or the type of butter you buy."

Jaden laughed. "The type of butter? Has that actually been an issue?"

"Yeah, I dated a guy who bought cheap butter that I couldn't eat. And he hated when I didn't record TV shows to skip over commercials."

Jaden walked around the counter. "Who gives a shit about those things?"

"I guess we did."

He turned her around on her stool. "Then you must have had a shitty sex life because if butter was more important than the guy, I don't know what to say."

She rested her hands on his shoulders. "I just think you get set in your ways, and there has to be a good reason to change. You told me at the steakhouse that you suck at relationships, but really, why didn't *you* ever get married?"

"I never fell in love. I liked a lot of women. And the sex was good. But I needed something deeper." Like what they once had. Maybe that had been the real problem. Other women weren't Keri.

"Wow, I like that answer. I guess I never fell in love either."

Lucky for him. Maybe he could change that. He kissed her forehead. "Selfishly, I'm glad you're still available. Now, I'm going to start shoveling snow. Wish me luck."

"The shovel is in the back where my horseshoes are, but you might want the snow blower instead."

"You have a snow blower? Oh man, you are so well prepared and didn't need me at all."

"Actually, Jaden, you might want to wait a while. It's super windy out there, and I don't want you to work, use up all the gas, and have the wind blow snow over the driveway again."

Staring out of the window, he realized she was right. "What should I do then?"

"Relax. Play a game on your phone. Watch videos."

"You're kidding. I don't do those things."

"Oh, you want to help me pack up the Christmas items?"

"Sure."

She went to the storage room and brought back boxes and packing materials. "This iPad here has the list of Christmas items that haven't sold and who they belong to. Take the items down. Pack them, then label the box with the artist's name."

"You don't plan to sell any more Christmas stuff?"

"I would have if I wasn't going with you to California. Once I return, it will be almost Christmas."

"True. No one wants to buy Christmas stuff after Christmas."

"Well, I close down for at least a month. When I reopen, I'll have the regular stuff back up." She crossed her arms and looked around. "Actually, let's do it together. I'll pull them off the shelves and walls, and you pack them. Would you mind bringing the ladder from the back so I can reach the art on the walls?"

"You got it." He whistled as he headed to her storeroom and found the ladder. Jaden couldn't remember feeling more satisfied than at this moment. Having spent the night making love to a gorgeous woman and now working beside her made him feel good in a way he couldn't describe.

He set the ladder down where she wanted it, and they started working. Keri climbed up and down a ladder, pulling paintings off the wall and handing them to him while he carefully wrapped and boxed them, writing the artist's name on the outside of the box. Then, he took them to the back to stack them where she wanted them stored.

He gripped the ladder and stared up at her, feeling a little like a pervert for noticing her bottom and fighting back the urge to touch her. "Shit, this is a lot of work. Do you normally do this on your own?"

"I have an assistant who comes in, but she has this week off." She handed him the last painting from the wall. "The rest is easier because it's on the floor or shelves."

He boxed the last painting, carried it to the back, and then returned to look out of the window. Placing his forehead on the glass, he blew and watched his breath fog the window. "Fuck this wind. When is it going to stop?"

Keri patted his back. "It will. Be patient. Are you hungry?"

"Yes, but I'm trying not to think about it."

She left his side and waved him back to the counter. "I have a bag of chips. An apple. A Kind bar. And a Greek yogurt that might still be good. This is all stuff I bring for lunch and never get around to eating. What would you like?"

He followed her to the counter. "You choose first."

"Hmm, okay, I'll take the yogurt."

"Good." He reached for the energy bar. "Your turn."

"You're doing all the physical work, and you need to go out in the snow soon. Eat the rest of it. I'm good with the yogurt."

He reached for the chips. "You eat the apple." Sitting on the floor and leaning on the counter, he ate the energy bar in three bites. Then he ripped open the Sun chips.

She sat beside him and spooned yogurt into her mouth. "Does your uncle know where you are?"

"Come to think of it, no. I should call him."

They sat in silence, finishing their snacks.

"So, when we get back, pack an overnight bag. I'll pick you up first thing in the morning. We need to be at the airport at about five."

"Should I pack anything in particular?"

"Yeah, something sexy."

She shook her head and smiled.

"Seriously, a cocktail dress. Sexy shoes. Your best lingerie."

Suddenly, they heard a loud crash in the back, and Keri jumped up and ran to the workroom. He followed. The wind had blown open her large barn-like doors.

"Shit," she said, charging outside without a jacket. She grabbed hold of one door and struggled to close it, but the wind knocked her off her feet and onto her back.

Jaden's heart leaped to his throat at seeing her thrown like a rag doll. He rushed to help her up while she released a string of curses. Together, they pushed the first door closed. "Can you hold it?" he asked.

She placed her back on the door and leaned on it. Jaden pulled the other door closed. The latch broke. She'd have to fix it and put a new one on, but not while the wind howled and snow blew around them. He looked around but didn't see anything that would hold the doors closed.

"Jaden, hold the doors. I'll go back inside and grab a hammer and nails. I have a couple of two-by-fours. We'll hammer them across for now to hold the doors shut."

"Okay."

"I'll unlock the front door so we can get back inside. And I'll bring your jacket."

"Thank you," he said.

He watched the powdery show blow around him. It was wild. Not a soul was around. No cars. Nothing. They were alone out here.

She returned quickly, and he was glad because he felt like a human icicle. She dropped the tools and two-by-fours on the ground and helped him into his jacket. Although she shivered, she picked up the wood and held it in place. "Can you hammer the nails in?"

He took the hammer. His hands were numb, but he drove the nails into the wood through to the doors. He placed one board on top and the second on the bottom.

Then he grabbed Keri's hand, and they ran to the front of the store. The wind made it challenging to move forward, but they reached the front of her store and got safely inside.

Keri trembled violently, and he was frozen as well. Breathing heavily, she stumbled to the back and brought back the electric heater. She also turned up the heat in the store. "Take your clothes off," she said.

"Yes, Ma'am," he winked, not really in the mood to joke but unable to resist. Keri took her clothes off, keeping on her burgundy bra and underwear and wrapped herself in blankets. She tossed him a blanket, too.

They sat on the floor by the heater facing each other.

"Well that was fun," he said as he defrosted. She looked worried.

"When the wind dies down, I'll add a new lock and brace it shut," he told her.

"I can do it. When the wind dies down, you'd better make a path to get a car out. Once they plow, we're going to want to leave. We'll still have a slow drive back. We'd also be better off taking my truck."

"True. I'll blow snow off your truck and get it ready." He leaned back. "For now, I think I'm going to take a nap."

"I can't sleep," she said. "But if you can, go ahead."

"Or we can have sex again," he said.

She laughed. "Right now, that would be too much effort. Go ahead and sleep. I'll wake you if the wind stops."

Wrapped in a blanket, he lay beside her and rested his head on her lap. She ran a hand through his hair, caressing his temples. He stared up at her as she brushed his hair back and massaged his head. His heart did a weird fluttering thing. "What are you thinking?" he asked, thinking of her sexy responses when he asked her that last night.

She shrugged. "That you look as content as Mochi does when I pet his head."

Jaden burst into laughter. "Great, she compares me to her dog."

With a smile, she shook her head. "I was really thinking about when we used to sit like this up on M Hill or by the lake. And how much I loved touching your silky hair."

He reached up and pulled her head down, kissing her, wanting her, wishing they could stay like this for the rest of his stay. She straightened and went back to playing with his hair. Surprisingly, it didn't take long for him to doze off. After a light night's sleep and freezing his butt off out there, he was tired.

When he opened his eyes, she was dressed again. She'd placed her blanket under his head. "How long have I been out?"

"A couple of hours. It's looking much better out there, which is good because it's going to be dark soon."

He stood and stretched, then dressed, and put on his hat, gloves, and jacket. Back out in the cold. "If I didn't have to back to California, and if I wasn't starving, I'd stay here another night." But he did have to leave, so he headed outside with the snow blower. He worked for about an hour and made it halfway to the main road. Then he blew the snow off of Keri's truck and went back inside to get warm.

"Man, that snow is deep," he said when he got back inside.

She gave him a cup of hot coffee that he gladly accepted.

"You made significant progress."

"They still haven't plowed the road this far, but I saw them working out there."

"I made another latch for the doors with my horseshoes," she said, showing him.

He raised an eyebrow. "Wow, you are one talented lady."

"When you go back out, I'll go with you and head back there to screw it in."

When Jaden finished his coffee, he trudged out to the cold outdoors. By the time he blew a path to the street, out in the distance, he saw a couple of snowplows working their way across. Satisfied, he walked back to the store. "Looks like we'll be able to leave soon. Did you secure those doors?"

Keri nodded. "It's done. I'll pack up."

She carried her bags and blankets to her truck. Then, she put a sign on the inside of her door letting customers know she would be closed until after Christmas and through January. About an hour later, the plows cleared the area in front of her store completely, and they were ready to make the trek back to Rapid City.

Keri turned all the lights off and locked the store. "Ready."

The drive wasn't as bad as they'd expected, and they arrived early enough to pick up a big bucket of fried chicken, mashed potatoes, macaroni and cheese, and coleslaw. Keri took Jaden to his uncle's house, and they ate dinner with him.

Uncle Frank gave Jaden hell for not calling.

"I meant to," he said between bites. "I'm sorry."

"Didn't you two have any food in that store?"

Jaden was eating his fifth piece of chicken and Keri her third. They each ate an entire Styrofoam container full of potatoes.

"Not really. We had a lot of coffee and fudge. I don't want to eat another piece of chocolate for a long time," Keri said.

"I figured you were with Keri," Uncle Frank said. "But I didn't know you went all the way out in Custer."

"He drove out to save me," she said, leaning over and dropping a kiss on Jaden's cheek. "My hero."

Uncle Frank raised a bushy eyebrow. "Hmm. I see."

She stood. "I'm going to go get my dog, take a long hot shower, and I'll pick you up in the morning, Jaden."

He swallowed the last of his chicken and stood.

"Don't walk me out. I'm good."

He wanted to give her a kiss goodbye but resisted. "Okay."

Keri did give Uncle Frank a kiss on his cheek. "Good night."

As soon as she was gone, Uncle Frank leaned over and slapped Jaden across the back of his head.

"Ouch, what did you do that for?"

"Because you never listen to me. You had to spend the night with her, didn't you? And now you're taking her to California?"

They'd told him their plan while scarfing up their dinner. "What is wrong with that?"

"What happens when this affair is over and you're ready to move on?"

Jaden stretched back and rubbed his stomach. "I love Keri. I've always loved Keri. I made a huge mistake ten years ago, and I'm not going to repeat it."

Uncle Frank frowned. "Meaning what?"

"Meaning I'm not going to lose her again. I will give her anything and everything she wants. You'll see."

"This is the craziest thing you've ever done," Keri's mom said.

"I know," she agreed. "But when will I have another chance to visit California? I decided, why not?"

Her mom gave her a skeptical look.

"So, will you keep Mochi for a few days? Please. I hate to ask, but I'm asking."

"He's no bother. He's here all the time anyway. Just be careful."

"I will be."

"Keri," she said, looking into Keri's eyes. "Never mind."

"Don't worry. We're just friends and having fun."

"Honey, he doesn't want to be your friend. And he tore your whole world apart last time. I don't want it to happen again."

"It's different this time," she said, not quite sure if she meant he was different, their relationship was different, or her expectations were. Maybe all of it was different.

Her mother gave her a hug. "You deserve to have fun and get away for a while. But you're too giving and trusting, and I worry. Don't mind me. It's my job as your mom to worry."

"Don't. Honestly. He can't hurt me. Because there's nothing I want from him."

Keri went home and did as she told Jaden. She took a luxuriously long, hot shower, then crawled into bed feeling amazing. And immediately, she fell asleep.

Early the following morning, they headed to the airport. Jaden had slept well but was wound up tight. He was excited about closing the deal on the car and excited about showing Keri his world.

He reached across as she drove and squeezed her thigh. "You're going to have a great time. And if you like California, maybe you'll come visit me for longer than a couple of days."

"Maybe," she shot him a quick look with a hint of a smile. "I'm excited to see the beach!"

"I'll definitely add it to our list of stops." He'd never been so willing to have a woman visit him. But Keri wasn't like other women.

He wanted her back, though he wasn't sure what that meant or how he was going to pull it off. But for once, he didn't feel like running. Quite the opposite. He wanted to be the guy who convinced her to run away from everything to be with him. And maybe the next few days would convince her to do just that.

CHAPTER TWENTY

Keri had watched the show "Amazing Race" a few times and now felt like she was one of the contestants. They had a relaxing flight in first class, where the flight attendants pampered them with drinks and food. Keri choose to drink only water and coffee, but she ate all the food they served because she wanted to enjoy every perk of this trip. When they landed, their relaxation ended, and they took off running. With their carry-ons rolling behind them, they made their way out of LAX.

Eduardo waited for them outside. They jumped into his car, and he hurried onto the freeway, where traffic slowed them down. But even with the packed freeway, they made it to Jaden's warehouse thirty minutes before his scheduled appointment.

"The car is ready to be lifted onto the truck. Once she inspects it, we'll get it delivered," Eduardo said. "The paperwork is on your desk."

Jaden high-fived him. "Beautiful. Thank you so much, man."

"Remember the spa day."

Jaden chuckled. "She'll get a card tomorrow with the invitation to schedule the date."

Eduardo nodded. "She will be a happy woman."

"You want to join her?"

"Do I look like I want to be kneaded like a loaf of bread? Naw, the kids and I will go do something fun, like eat pizza." He turned to Keri. "Nice to meet you. Did your dad like his car?"

"He did. Thank you for delivering it."

"No problem."

Keri strolled around the warehouse, impressed by the cars. Once Eduardo left, Jaden, opened the driver door to a Lamborghini. "Want to sit inside?"

She slid behind the wheel, captivated with the luxury, but not convinced that it was worth what people paid for these things. "Are we going to drive one?"

"Not these. They have to be pristine." He held out a hand to help her out. "But we'll take one of mine for a drive."

"How many cars do you have?"

"Four and one truck and a motorcycle that I don't use anymore. Drivers are crazy. One almost knocked me into another car once."

"Hmm," she walked around the car. "So, tell me really, what was up with giving one of your cars to my dad? Was it just to . . . get close to me?"

Jaden placed his fingers in his front pocket and angled his head. "There was this guy, an influencer, and he really wanted a Ferrari to take pictures in front of and post online. These young guys, they're full of it, okay. They want to look the part."

"The part?"

"Yeah, rich, you know. They want to pretend they've made it when they haven't really." He shrugged. "I get it. I was there once. So anyway, he didn't have the money. He was about fifteen thousand short, so he offered me his car." Jaden spread his arms out. "I knew I could sell it for twenty if I had to, so I accepted it as partial payment. But I don't have the kind of buyers who would ever want the car."

"But you could have sold it. You're in the business. You could have found a buyer."

He strolled toward her. "I drove it for a while, but it wasn't my style. Like I said, I have five vehicles. So, the damn thing sat here taking up space." Stopping beside her, he lifted her chin. "I wanted to do something nice to help out a good, hardworking man that I cared about a lot when I was younger."

"And?"

"And, that's it?"

"I shouldn't feel manipulated."

"Hell no. It's a write-off for me. Trust me, I need the tax benefit of a loss. Now, I don't have to pay registration fees anymore or keep in here."

She placed her fingers on the waistband of his jeans. "I believe you. I don't know about trust yet."

A woman cleared her voice. "I hate to interrupt."

"Hey, Bethany." He stepped back. "Let's go to my office. Keri, you want to come with us?"

Keri shook her head. "I'll wait here."

He disappeared with the beautiful blond who dressed in a tight dress like she was going to a party. Keri stepped outside to soak up the California sun. Here it was almost Christmas, and it was in the seventies in Los Angeles. She didn't think she'd like that. But she took a picture of the palm trees and sent it to Sam.

Immediately, she received a text asking where she was. Keri laughed and explained her wild, last-minute decision.

Sam texted: "I really don't get what's going on between you two."

"Neither do I," Keri texted back. "But he showed up at my store in a snowstorm, acting like a knight in shining armor. Then he asked me to fly to California, and it just sounded like fun, so I said yes. Now, here I am."

Keri didn't share what happened between them. She wasn't ready to talk about that.

"Have fun and tell me all about it when you come back."

She promised she would and went back inside to sit on the comfortable couch, positioned to take in the view of his cars. She almost dozed off as she waited in the large, quiet warehouse.

When Jaden and Bethany emerged from the office, they were both laughing and happy. She kissed his cheek and strolled toward the exit. She waved her fingers at Keri. "Have a good night. He's all yours again."

As soon as Bethany drove away, Jaden punched the air. "Yes! Done. Now," he reached for her hand and pulled her up. "Ms. Artiest, I'm taking you to the Getty, then on a dinner cruise in Marina del Rey. They have a holiday cruise that is fabulous. I've already called and made reservations. Ready?"

"Wow, yeah. Am I dressed okay?"

"Mm, you brought a cocktail dress?"

"Yes. I didn't know if you were serious about that, so I packed one just in case."

"Good, you can change after we leave the Getty. The dinner cruise will be a little dressy, but it will get cool out on the water. Nothing compared to what we just left, of course."

He led her to a car parked in a separate garage. "This is one of my non-luxury cars. I'm not much for muscle cars, but this one is an exception. It's a 1969 Ford Mustang Boss 429."

"It looks like an old burgundy car."

With a big grin, he nodded. "That it is. But this beauty has all original parts and only 23,000 miles. It's my baby. Get in."

She slipped inside. Jaden closed the door and got in behind the wheel on the driver sided.

"It's very pretty," Keri said. "Now, this is something my dad would have driven when he was young."

"Probably something like it. Even in 69, there were only 1359 of these cars made. It's pretty rare. Back then, this car would have run about $4700, which was pricy. Today, I could get $420,000 for this car in this condition."

Kari's jaw dropped. "For this old car."

He laughed and started the engine. "Yep."

"Oh my God, I would be afraid to drive it."

"It does make me a little nervous, and I don't drive it all the time."

"What were you driving when you got in your accident?"

"A rental, thankfully. Any one of my cars would have been tragic to lose."

They reached the Getty Museum in about thirty minutes, and during the drive, Jaden told her stories about the Brentwood area.

"You seem so comfortable here, really at home."

"It's my home when I'm not traveling. I love it."

"I can see why."

"There's always something interesting to do."

They spent a couple of hours walking around, enjoying the European paintings and drawings. The grounds, with the gardens and the buildings themselves, were the most amazing pieces of art. When The Getty closed at five-thirty, Keri wasn't really ready to leave, but they had to get to the dinner cruise.

Jaden pulled into a Starbucks where they changed clothes in the bathroom and bought a coffee each. "Mm," Keri said. "This hits the spot. I need a little pick-me-up."

They arrived at the beautifully lit marina, magically decorated for Christmas. They settled on the boat, each with a glass of wine, enjoying the night out on the harbor, waiting to pull out. The day felt like a whirlwind, and though she was tired, Jaden seemed to pick up energy as the night progressed. Evidently, he thrived in this high-octane lifestyle.

Soon after the yacht pulled out, Keri stood at the railing to enjoy the slap of the water hitting the boat. Because it was so dark, she couldn't see much of the ocean, but when she looked back, the marina's lights twinkled.

Jared stood behind her, placing his arms on top of the railing and encircling her body. "What are you thinking?"

She laughed. "Are you going to keep making fun of me for asking you that question during sex?"

"I'm not making fun of you. I really want to know."

"I wasn't thinking about anything really, just enjoying being out here. It's so peaceful compared to the craziness of the city."

"Yep, it's an amazing contrast, isn't it? Southern California is full of them. You can be in the city in the morning, the ocean in the afternoon, the desert in the evening, the mountains late at night."

The breeze blew her hair, and though many tourists might be cold, this was perfect for her. "Thanks for bringing me." She turned to her side to face him.

"Thanks for coming." He placed a hand on her hip and moved closer. "I never thought I'd see you again, much less have you visit me." She expected him to kiss her, but he gazed into her eyes for a few seconds and then looked out at the water.

Once they got out far enough for the yacht to stop and float, the crew served dinner and played music. Jaden and Keri ate, danced a little to soft romantic instrumental music, talked about nothing important, and Keri loved it all. She would file it all away and remember it once she was back home, and he left and came back to his life here.

Jaden was excited to take her to his home. It wasn't anything super special. Every home in this area was a million-plus dollar home, and his place had cost him three, but it was small compared to others in the neighborhood. He only had four bedrooms and a couple of bathrooms, but he bought it for the land. He built a garage that was as large as his house to store his vehicles. And he had a private entrance and an amazing view of Los Angeles.

When Keri walked in, her jaw dropped. "Wow, Jaden. Just wow," she said, walking to the living room floor to ceiling sliding glass door and looking out at the city in the distance.

He stepped up behind her. "I have a pool out in the backyard and a basketball court. I'm sort of in the hills, which is nice, but of course, it's nothing like the Black Hills."

"Ah, no. Not with all those palm trees."

"When I saw the view, and that it was sort of secluded up here, I knew this was the place I wanted."

She turned away from the glass door and walked around the room. He'd paid to get it decorated since he didn't have any decorating style at all. He wondered what she thought.

"How many cars did you have to sell to afford something like this?"

He laughed and dropped onto his couch, patting the spot beside him. "A lot. I move about twenty cars a month."

"I'm really happy that you've been so successful," she said, sitting beside him and curling her legs to the side. "Because I know it makes *you* happy."

Having her here in his house felt surreal but right. He didn't bring women to his home often, almost never. Friends, sometimes. He had parties occasionally, but mostly, it was his private escape. He leaned in and brushed her lips with his, then kissed the tip of her nose, and her temple. Pulling back, he gazed into her eyes. "Are you tired?"

She nodded.

"Want to see my bedroom? Or . . . would you like to stay in a guest bedroom?"

Her lips curved. "You're giving me a choice?"

"Of course. I'm not making any assumptions."

"Show me your bedroom."

He took her arm and led her upstairs. When they walked in, she took a moment to fully appreciate his spacious bedroom; she glanced through the French door, taking in the breathtaking view from the balcony, before pivoting to face him. "I love your house," she said.

He cupped her face and kissed her, walking her gently back until they reached his bed. He wanted to make love to her the right way this time, not on a hard floor.

Slipping his hands under her dress, he caressed her thighs, her hips, her belly. And she unbuttoned his shirt, easing it off his shoulders and kissing his chest.

Slowly, they continued to explore each other's bodies silently. She ran her fingers along his ribcage and slid them up his back and along his spine. He cupped her breast that looked perfectly adorned in that dress and pinched her nipples to make them push against her bra and silky dress. He was so turned on. But he took a step back and pulled the blankets back as an invitation, which she accepted and slid under the covers. He wanted to be inside of her, to slowly bring her to climax.

He opened a nightstand drawer and pulled out a little packet. "Look what I have this time."

She laughed. "A condom? A little too late for that, don't you think?"

With a shrug, he handed it to her. "I don't know. I hope not?"

She reached across to where he stood beside the bed, got on her knees and unhooked his slacks, then slowly lowered the zipper, making his dick swell. "You hope not? You're not sure?"

Keri was perfect, and he wanted her back—not for the Christmas season, not for a few weekends a year. But he'd decided he was never going to give her up again. He didn't want a kid, though—at least not yet.

She eased his slacks and boxers down and peeled open the condom packet. She scooted closer to slip it on him but instead, took him into her mouth. He gasped at the unexpected pleasure. "Oh, man," he said, placing a hand on her head as he watched the erotic scene unfold and tried not to embarrass himself by coming early. He tried to recite the list of cars he owned. *Think of something else,* he told himself. But it felt so damned intense. "Keri, enough," he said and eased her back. He breathed as if he'd run up the stairs. Beads of perspiration covered his forehead.

"I couldn't resist," she said, gazing up at him. "You looked so enticing."

He ran a hand through his hair and stepped out of his pants and boxers. She was still fully dressed in that hot dress and shoes, but not for long. He slid her dress up to her hips and ran his hands up her legs. "How does a woman who fights a snow storm like a champ look so feminine and sexy a few days later?"

She lay back on his pillows and smiled. "Real women can do it all."

He reached for her panties and slid them down her legs. "I believe it. You can do it all." She looked so hot in that dress, waiting for him on his bed. Damn, he wanted her now. "Wrap your legs around me."

She did, but as he straddled her, she placed her fingers on his stomach. "The condom," she said. She pulled it out of the packet and placed it on the tip of his penis. But he slapped it out of her fingers.

"Ouch," she said. "What did you do that for?"

"Fuck the condom."

"You don't want it now?"

He positioned himself between her legs and entered her body, releasing a groan in ecstasy. "No more donor sperm, Keri. You understand?"

She draped her arms around him. "Don't do this to sleep with me. It can affect the rest of your life. Go get the condom."

But he wasn't listening to her. All he wanted was to bring her pleasure. He moved inside her, taking her lips and plunging his tongue hungrily in a passionate kiss. And within seconds, she had forgotten the condom, lost in their lovemaking.

After a scream that told him he'd succeeded in his goal, he sank deep inside her, and his body spasmed, sending him into a thrill ride no race car could match.

They lay spent, side by side. Finally, she got on her side and leaned over him. "Jaden, about the condom and repercussions of —."

"I don't want to talk about that."

"It's kind of important."

"I'm okay with whatever happens. You've made up your mind that you want to get pregnant, and I sure as hell don't want you to keep getting inseminated with another guy's sperm."

She frowned and seemed to consider this. "Okay, I'll stop doing that. But we should use a condom. At least for now. Okay?"

"Why?"

"Do you want to be a dad? Be honest."

"Honest?"

She nodded, looking so beautiful that he didn't want to disappoint her. "I want to make you happy. I want to give you anything that will make you happy."

She caressed his face. "That's sweet. But do *you* want to be a dad?"

Sighing, he shook his head. "Not really, but —."

"Then, let's be careful from now on. Just for a little while."

He sat up. "Just until you see if I'm going to stick around? Is that what you're saying?"

"I'm perfectly willing to be a mom without any guy, but I'm starting to get the feeling you wouldn't be okay with that. You'd feel obligated to help raise it."

"You're right. I wouldn't let you raise my baby alone."

She looked around his room. "You have a life here. I'm not part of it."

"You can be."

But she shook her head, crushing his hopes of making her a part of his life.

Well, at least now he knew where he stood. If he wanted her, he'd have to go to her. He pulled her into his arms and held her. Well, damn.

CHAPTER TWENTY-ONE

K eri woke up late. Yesterday had been exhausting, exciting, fun, sexy, and revealing. Jaden, this new incarnation of Jaden, was so different from the one she used to know. She could never fit into his life. She was still a simple girl, and he lived in a world that was intense, and though she wasn't judging it, it wasn't for her.

And yet, it felt so perfect being with him. Their lovemaking, the second time, lasted for a couple of hours as he slowly kissed and explored every inch of her body, and she did the same. It was a getting to know each other again experience.

"Here you go," he handed her a pair of his running shorts and a T-shirt. We'll swing by a store on the way to the beach so you can buy a swimsuit and clothes that actually fit you."

She took it. "I brought jeans and t-shirts, but no shorts or swimsuit."

"You want to go for a swim now? You don't need a swimsuit. No one can look into my backyard."

"Swim naked? I can't do that."

He shrugged. "Let's get ready to go, then. We're headed back tonight, so let's not waste the day."

Keri stood and wrapped her arms around him. "Slow down a little."

"I'm eager to show you as much as I can," he said, like an impatient little boy.

"Okay, but I'm enjoying this, too. Being here with you, replacing old memories with these new ones. When I'm in South Dakota, I want to think of you here in your beautiful house doing a job that you love."

"Why does it feel like you're saying goodbye? I'm going back with you."

"I know. But after the holidays, you'll return here and be you, and I'll stay home and be me."

He frowned. "But things have changed with us. Right?"

"Not really. I mean, I don't hate you anymore. Not too much anyway." She winked.

"That's progress." He patted her butt. "Let's go."

They spent the day at the beach, which was amazing. Jaden rubbed suntan lotion all over her body, insisting she needed it. She thought he was just doing it to run his hands over every intimate curve. Blushing, she slapped his hands away. He simply laughed. Though the day was overcast, she got a little sunburnt, so she really did need sunblock protection.

They held hands and walked up and down the beach. He chased her in and out of the surf, and she felt like she was sixteen again. The day evaporated so quickly that, before she knew it, they were back at his place to shower and change to catch a flight home.

Jaden insisted on showering together in his large, spectacular shower full of jets and waterfalls and argued that she had to have sex with him one more time in the shower.

"We're going to be late," she'd said.

"I don't care." He pinned her against the shower wall. "After watching you all day on the beach in that sexy bikini, I've had to endure a five-hour erection. You don't have a choice here, Keri. You did this to me," he teased.

She touched said erection, running her fingertips along the front of it, and he closed his eyes and moaned.

"You're making me feel very powerful," she said and kissed his chin.

"You have no idea the power you have." Moving her hand away, he pressed his pelvis against hers. "I'm going to have hot, quick sex with you. And you're going to love it."

She laughed. "Am I now? I'm going to start thinking that you're a sex addict."

He lifted one of her legs and pressed his hips into hers, entering smoothly and in one thrust.

She gasped and was about to remind him about the condom, but she let it go. Something told her that he wasn't going to bother with it, and she hoped he didn't come to regret it once the passion faded.

"Only with you. I can't get enough," he said, already lost in desire.

And to prove it, he pumped quickly and hard. The intensity of his possession as he deeply entered her made her unable to catch her breath. She was beautifully trapped, her back to the shower wall. His fingers gripped her leg, encouraging her to curl it around him, while his other hand curved around her waist. She couldn't have moved if she wanted to, and what woman in her right mind would want to?

Instead, she surrendered to what his body was doing to hers, her hands resting lightly on his chest, mesmerized by the sight of him. His head was thrown back as he thrust repeatedly, exposing the chords of his neck and the strength of his jaw. The muscles in his neck stood out, taut and defined, highlighting the primal intensity that radiated from him. Watching him in this moment of raw desire, his eyes closed, lost in masculine pleasure, ignited an equally deep desire within her that sent her over the edge. Keri cried out as an overwhelming orgasm hit her. He gripped her against him as he joined her in his own explosive moment of ecstasy. He slid down the wall with Keri wrapped around him. Water fell over them, making it feel like they were under a natural waterfall. It was sexy, purely erotic, unforgettable magic.

She could barely breathe, barely think. What in the world was that?

"Ugh, Keri, I love being with you," he said, kissing her forehead, her temple, her neck. "How the hell have I lived without you the last ten years?"

She hugged him close and let her head fall on his shoulder, unwilling to voice the complex feelings in her heart.

Being back in Rapid City, listening to his uncle snore in his bedroom, made Jaden happy. Just the couple of days in L.A. made him realize how empty and shallow his life had become. Not that he didn't love the world he'd created for himself and his business. It all filled him with electric energy and a pulse that was vital. He felt alive when he was in the center of the action, but it required him to be on all the time. Here, he could relax; he could just be.

Unable to sleep, he got out of bed. At five in the morning, the sky was still dark. Christmas lights on neighborhood homes twinkled, and it was so quiet that he felt like the only human on earth. Every once in a while, he heard the trains honking, which was the only indication that there was life out there.

He got dressed, put on gloves, a hat, and a jacket, and went to sit outside on the porch, watching his breath escape and evaporate. "What am I going to do about Keri?" he asked himself.

"Who are you talking to?" his uncle's grumpy voice came from the door behind him. The door creaked, and the old man came to sit beside him.

"To the stars, I guess."

"What's wrong?"

"Nothing."

"You're out here freezing your ass off for some reason.

"Just couldn't sleep and wanted some fresh air. I might go for a run when the sun comes up."

Frank quietly waited for him to say more.

"You think I can convince Keri to move with me to California?"

"Nope. I was surprised she agreed to go for a couple of days."

"She loved it."

"Hmm. I hear she loves her business and her parents and her town and—."

"I could give her more."

Frank scratched his head, pulled his beanie further down his head, and hugged his arms around his body. "Really? What are you going to give that girl?"

"Whatever she wants?"

"Why?"

"Because I can. She could have the best cars, a way better house than the place she's renting now, amazing clothes, European vacations. Great sex." He grinned. "What can't I give her?"

"Well," Uncle Frank said. "Now that you've asked let me share something I've learned about women."

"You've learned something? Is that why you're still living alone?"

"Yes, smart ass, I have. Women don't care about any of that stuff."

"The women I've dated *only* care about that stuff," Jaden said. They would have married him in a heartbeat if he'd asked.

"I'm sure," Uncle Frank said. "Sensible women, like this one that you seem to be infatuated with, only want one thing, and you haven't mentioned it yet."

"Yeah, I know. Kids."

Frank frowned. "Not kids, you idiot. Love."

"Oh." He gazed out in the distant sky at the stars that twinkled brighter than the fake lights on Earth. "I've loved her since the first moment I saw her in seventh grade."

"Then that changes things, but I still don't think she's going to leave everything she knows for . . . ."

"A guy who left her once already?"

"Maybe I'm wrong." Frank stood. "It's too cold for me out here. I'll let you keep thinking about this."

"I want to give her the best Christmas she's ever had."

"That's a good start. How are you going to do that?"

"I don't know yet."

Uncle Frank patted his shoulder. "You're a good boy. You always have been. Your mom would have been proud of you."

He thought of the box in the garage. "She would have been proud of you too, Uncle Frank. You gave up everything for me."

"It was worth it." He slipped inside.

Jaden wiped at his eyes, which had grown misty. He stood and walked east to watch the sunrise. "What can I do to make Christmas special for you, Keri?"

Keri met her friends for drinks the night after she returned from California. She had slept all day, and when she woke up, she had a dozen messages from her friends. Drinks and loud music suited her fine.

Once they all ordered, they began shooting questions at her. What happened? Why did you go with him? What is going on?

Keri shook her head and put her hands up. "Jaden made the best decision ever by leaving me. He lives like a king in a gorgeous house on a hill with the most amazing views of Los Angeles. He has ridiculously expensive cars. And I'm sure he can sleep with any woman he wants?"

"Including you?" Sam asked.

"That," Keri said, "is none of your business."

Her friends laughed.

"No way, you are not getting away with that," Sam said. "Tell us everything."

"Yeah," Amanda said. "Did you accomplish your goal or not? Is he into you again?"

"Was that my goal?"

"That's what I thought. Wasn't that the game?"

Keri shook her head. If it was, she was the big loser. Or winner? She was the one who'd given her heart again. Not that he didn't like her and want her. He obviously did. "Here's the truth. We had a good time. And, yes, the goal has been met."

Amanda and Sam cheered. Jenn didn't say much.

Keri shared pictures she took in California, and afterward, thankfully, they changed the subject. They were having fun, but they were starting to make her feel uncomfortable. This wasn't a game. Even though she hadn't wanted to, she cared about Jaden again. Maybe she was stupid, maybe she'd opened herself up to get hurt again. They had no future, but she couldn't help it. He was easy to...care about. She shook thoughts of Jaden away and focused on the discussion that had moved to Christmas dinners and recipes.

CHAPTER TWENTY-TWO

J aden stood in front of the jeweler in the mall. The display cases were filled with glittering rings of all sizes and shapes, and the bright mall lights illuminated the silver, gold, and diamond settings.

Although he'd taken off his jacket and sweater, he was sweating. None of the rings looked good enough. Keri wouldn't want something too extravagant; it wasn't her style. But he didn't want to pick something too simple, either. The saleswoman showed him practically everything she had.

"Choose something you like, and if she doesn't like that style, she can always come back and choose something else."

"I'm making it too hard." He also wasn't one hundred percent sure he was doing the right thing. He'd proposed once before, and then he'd left. And now, wasn't he going to do the same thing? Not leave her, but he couldn't live here, could he? Would he be able to move his business? His clients lived in big cities. He pointed to a ring with an oval diamond on a white gold band with a twist frame that held tiny diamonds.

"Good choice," the saleslady said. What else was she going to say?

As she rang up the sale, cheerful Christmas music and bustling shoppers surrounded Jaden, providing constant background noise to accompany his anxious thoughts. He wanted to propose because he loved her; he wanted her to be his forever. This wasn't like when he was younger, when he'd proposed out of a desperate attempt to hold on to her.

He paid and walked away with the ring in his pocket. Was he really going to do this? Would this make it the happiest Christmas ever for her?

As he strolled the mall, looking for other things to buy her, a woman waved at him.

"Hey Jaden, it's Jenn. Remember me from Brady's birthday party? Ice skating? You bought us hot chocolate?"

"Of course. How are you?"

"Crazy. Last minute shopping. How about you?"

"Same. Do you happen to know Keri's favorite perfume?"

"You know, I'm not really sure. I think she uses a type of Chanel, but I'm not sure which one. Smell them and choose one that you like."

"That's a good idea." He'd probably recognize it if he smelled it. He could smell Keri from across the room.

"So . . . how are things going with you two? She had a fabulous time in California."

Jaden couldn't hold back a grin, encouraged that Keri had mentioned the trip to her friends. "I'm glad she had fun." That's all he planned to say about their relationship.

"She did. I guess this means . . . all is good with you both again?"

He wasn't sure how much Keri had said to her friends. "I think she's forgiven me for the past, so yeah, all is good."

Jenn gave him a bright smile. "I'm so glad. I guess this means she hasn't invited you to the New Year's Eve party."

"Ah, no."

"Good."

"Good?" Jaden wasn't sure what to say about that.

"Yes, great! It means she's really changed her mind about you." She paused. "Wait, she told you about the whole little revenge thing, right?"

Jaden had absolutely no idea what this woman was talking about, but he nodded.

"It was silly," Jenn said. "Honestly, I thought it was childish and mean."

"Right," Jaden said. "Childish."

"Not that you wouldn't have deserved to be humiliated in front of all our friends after breaking her heart the way you did when you left her," Jenn said playfully. "But that was so long ago."

This was getting interesting. "I probably would have deserved it. But what does New Year's Eve have to do with it?"

"That's where she was going to break off whatever little thing you two have going. Dump you in front of everyone, all her friends, and those who remember you." Jenn angled her head. "You said she told you."

"Oh, is that where it was supposed to happen?" He remembered Keri saying that if he fell for her, it would be humiliating for him. Was that what she meant?

"Yeah, but I'm glad she changed her mind. You seemed really nice at Brady's party, and like you were really into her. I didn't like their dumb plan. You both deserve to be happy."

Jaden nodded, his neck and shoulders tensing, growing angry the more Jenn shared with him. He wondered who she meant when she said 'their plan,' but most likely, Sam was involved in this. She never made it a secret how she felt about him. "It was good to see you, Jenn."

"Good to see you, too. And I'm glad it worked out with you two."

As she left, Jaden stood rooted in the middle of the mall, wondering what the hell this meant. Had their whole relationship been fake, just a game Keri was playing with him? No fucking way. She slept with him. Multiple times. But Jenn said that Keri had changed her mind, which meant it had started as a revenge scheme, and that still pissed him off.

He left the mall and started driving to Keri's house. Halfway there, he slammed on the brakes and turned around, returning to Uncle Frank's house. Right now, he was too angry to talk to Keri. He needed to calm down and think.

That night, she called him, and he turned his phone off. He sat watching TV with Uncle Frank, not seeing or hearing anything, seething. His uncle seemed to sense that he was in a bad mood and left him alone.

He couldn't believe she planned to dump him. How fucked up was that? Here, he'd been trying to beg her forgiveness and make her happy, and she'd been dating him only to break up with him. It was so unlike the woman he'd fallen in love with.

And at what point had she changed her mind, exactly? Before or after she slept with him? She sure as hell seemed to enjoy having sex with him, even though she didn't want to hear any promises about the future. She flat-out told him she wouldn't even consider a relationship. She was going to return here and be her, and he was going to stay in California and be him, she said. Maybe she wasn't going to dump him publicly, but she planned to dump him. It was clear now. She'd told him repeatedly that this relationship was temporary. And he bought her a ring. What a fucking idiot he was.

He was partially to blame for this. He didn't listen. All he could think of was how he felt and what he wanted because he so badly wanted her. Wrapped up in falling in love, and enjoying the very real sexual spark between them, he failed to hear what she was actually saying.

The next day was the twenty-third of December. He and Frank went to see his doctor. True to his word, Uncle Frank made an appointment to check on his shakiness and dizzy spells. Jaden was glad to go and focus on something other than Keri. The doctor ordered blood tests and checked Uncle

Frank's blood pressure again to ensure that he had the right prescription. The basic check-up verified that Uncle Frank was doing okay but that he had to watch his diet.

"See?" Jaden said. "You believe me now?"

"I already knew that." He grumbled. "I just don't want to eat salad all the time."

The doctor gave him healthier eating options that did not include eating strictly salads.

When they left the clinic, they stopped at the grocery store to buy food for Christmas Eve.

"Thanks for going with me," Uncle Frank said. "And for worrying about me. But you don't have to, you know?"

"Okay. Just promise to take better care of yourself."

When they got back home, Jaden sat outside. The porch had three steps. Jaden sat at the top, his forearms rested on his knees, and he stared out at the trees, listening to birds sing like there was something to celebrate.

So, what now? He didn't know. He no longer felt angry with Keri, but instead felt deflated. Honestly, he wanted to cry like a little boy. If only he could; maybe he'd feel better. He rubbed his face with both hands, scratching his fingers back across his scalp.

His uncle opened the storm door. "Hey, since you're out there, you want to chop some firewood so we can have a fire tonight and on Christmas Eve?

"Sure," Jaden agreed.

Taking an ax to trunks of wood sounded perfect. He needed to pound the hell out of something. He ended up cutting all the wood his uncle had outside and stacking it neatly in the woodpile he had behind his house. As he came around the front, Keri walked toward him.

His heart stopped. She was so beautiful. It hurt so much to want something you couldn't have.

"Hey," she said.

"Hey, Keri."

"How have you been? I've been calling."

"Yeah, I saw. I had my phone off."

"Why?"

"I didn't want to be bothered."

She half frowned and half smiled, looking confused. She stepped closer. "I see." Coming to a stop in front of him, she said, "Actually, I don't see. Is something wrong?"

"What could be wrong?"

"I don't know."

"Are you here to invite me to the New Year's Eve party?"

"What New Year's Eve . . . oh, that party? With my friends?"

He gripped his ax harder. "Yeah, *that* party? Am I invited?" His breath swirled between them. He waited for her to admit what she had planned, to fill him in, to explain.

"Sure," she said. "You're invited. Who told you about that party?"

"I saw your friend, Jenn, at the mall yesterday."

Keri nodded, understanding.

"I'm wondering why you didn't tell me."

"I didn't . . . think. I didn't think you'd want to go."

He huffed. "Oh, no. I want to go. I wouldn't want to spoil your plan."

"Listen, Jaden. Forget about the party. I really wanted to invite you and your uncle to my parents' house for Christmas Eve. That's why I was calling. We'd love to have you."

Jaden's jaw tightened, and he looked up at the snow-covered pine trees on his uncle's property. He wanted to ask her how she really felt about him. He wanted to know the truth. But he gazed at her, and he knew. He'd held her in his arms as she passionately called out his name, and she'd gazed deeply into his eyes conveying without words what she felt. He knew Keri had grown to care about him again. But she'd been so angry that she'd started this whole relationship to try to hurt him. And she had succeeded. "Naw, thanks, Keri. We're going to spend it alone, just the two of us."

"Are you sure?" she said, her voice sounding sad and confused.

His heart ached. "I'm sure."

Gazing at him, she said, "Jaden." She took a step closer, and he stepped back.

"It's been nice spending the last couple of weeks with you. Spectacular really. But I'm headed back home right after Christmas."

"Oh."

They stared at each other. Nothing left to say. Unless she asked him not to go. Unless she admitted that she loved him. Her eyes were bright with unshed tears until she broke eye contact, bit her lower lip, and shook her head.

"Merry Christmas, Keri." He turned away, placed the ax on the porch, and went inside. A few seconds later, he heard the car drive off.

Uncle Frank watched him from his chair in the living room. "What the hell happened, Boy?"

Jaden's eyesight blurred. "She faked this entire relationship because she wanted to get back at me for leaving her ten years ago."

"That doesn't sound like something she'd do."

"Yeah, well, she fooled us both."

"You don't think she cares about you?"

"She doesn't want me," Jaden raised his voice and immediately felt bad. "I'm sorry." He held an open hand out to stop his questions. "Not permanently. I guess all she wanted was a fling, a little fun. Now, it's over."

"If I were you, I'd hear her out. Maybe you're wrong."

Jaden shook his head. He didn't want advice or to hear anyone out. "Listen, I'm going to go for a drive. I need to think." He ran a hand through his hair and looked down at the table for his keys, not seeing them.

"If you need space, do what you need to do."

Jaden felt angry and caged, just like when he was younger. He didn't want to be here, not even for Christmas. He'd bought Uncle Frank a gift Keri had created. Now, he didn't want to see him open it. "I'm sorry. I'll be back for Christmas. I promise. I just don't want to be here right now."

He stormed into his bedroom. On his nightstand, he saw his car keys and the ring he was going to give Keri on Christmas Eve. He picked them both up and put them in his pocket. He gave his uncle a long hug, not wanting to let him go, but wanting to run, to get away from this town that had done nothing but bring him pain. Getting into the car, he wasted no time stepping on the gas and skidding out of the driveway.

Quickly, he drove out of town. He wasn't sure where he was going, but he headed into the hills toward Custer, where he'd rushed to save Keri from a snowstorm. Jaden pressed the accelerator down even more, taking a few curves a little too fast. He told himself to slow down and had weird images of his last accident, of lying unconscious in the totaled car. Cursing, he picked up more speed.

Maybe he'd drive for days. Drive all the way back to California. His uncle would understand, wouldn't he?

Hear her out, Uncle Frank said. Hear what? Hear her say again that they had different lives, that all she wanted was a one-night stand or a holiday romance? Plus, he gave her the opportunity to tell him what was going on, and she didn't. She just stood there looking hurt. Well, this time, it was her damned fault. He'd been honest and open and real.

He took another curve too fast, and the car slid, but he righted it and kept going. Damn it. Was he angry at her or at himself for even thinking of changing his whole life, everything he'd spent ten years building, for a woman? Even this woman.

Or was he honestly just scared? Was he running again? He thought of lying beside her in her store, wanting her with every fiber of his being, and her words, *"The only way you were ever going to lose me was by leaving me."* Was that still true?

Shit, what was he doing? Keri loved him. She always had. She was just afraid to trust him. It had taken her time to come to terms with their past. And what had he done? He'd taken her to California to impress her, and all he'd accomplished was to show her how absolutely wrong they were for each other. When all along, he should have told her he was willing to leave it all for her.

"Fuck!" He hit the steering wheel, slammed on the brakes, and made a U-turn.

He sensed more than felt the tires go over black ice, and suddenly, the car was sliding, skating across the road. He turned the wheel helplessly, trying to regain control as the car went off the road, and the passenger side hit a tree at full force, crushing that side of the car and cracking the left side of his head into the door window. The impact knocked Jaden into the steering wheel airbag, and crushing pain to his ribs took his breath away.

Suddenly, he was standing in a hospital — a large white room — and a guy with a clipboard walked toward him.

CHAPTER TWENTY-THREE

K eri maneuvered her truck through the winding roads that led to Jenn's house, her grip on the steering wheel tightening with each turn as she wondered what Jenn had said to send Jaden running back to California. The sun dipped below the horizon, casting an angry red hue over the quaint neighborhood as she pulled up in front of Jenn's home.

Keri grabbed her purse and slammed the truck's door shut, telling herself to calm down. She marched up the recently shoveled and icy concrete walk and impatiently pounded on Jenn's front door. The porch light flickered before Jenn opened the door.

Her kids were eating popcorn and watching a Christmas animated movie while Paul was in the garage building a couple of bikes to put under the tree on Christmas morning. Jenn gave her a hug. "This a surprise! Give me your coat."

Keri waved her away. "I'm not staying. I just want to know what you said to Jaden."

"About what?"

"I don't know. He seemed really upset, and he asked me about the New Year's Eve party."

"Oh that. I was just curious if you'd mentioned it to him, and he said that you had."

"I never talked to him about the party. I wasn't even going to go."

Jenn looked confused. "He said that you'd told him all about your revenge game. Are you sure you don't want to come in?"

"No, I don't. How could he say that? I was never playing a game with him. I would never tell him that."

"I'm sorry, Keri. We all thought that was why you were dating him, to get even. That's what you told us every time we got together."

Keri rubbed her temples. "So, you told him *what* exactly?"

Jenn looked away like she was thinking. "That I was glad you'd changed your mind. That . . . I don't even remember. It didn't seem like a big deal because he said he knew. He was in the mall buying you a gift. I didn't think I was revealing anything. I'm really sorry."

Keri shook her head. "It's my fault. I should have made it clear to you guys that the little joke was just that. I need to go talk to him and apologize."

"I'm sorry, Keri. I feel bad. I shouldn't have said anything. I guess I was trying to gauge how serious things were with you two. I shouldn't have been so nosy."

"I fell in love with him all over again. Does that answer your question? And I thought he'd fallen in love with me. But he basically told me it was over after finding out about this dumb non-plan to hurt him."

"Oh, hell. I'm so sorry. Go tell him how you feel."

Keri left and hurried back to Frank's house, hoping Jaden would talk to her and understand that it had all been dumb girl talk, and that it had been before she'd gotten to know him again.

When she knocked on Frank's door, she sheepishly asked if she could come inside. Frank stepped aside.

"If you're here to see Jaden, he's gone."

What did he mean gone? "When is he coming back?"

"Next year? In five years? Never?" Frank sat in his chair with a grunt. "You know how he is. Sit." He pointed to the couch across from him.

Keri took a seat. "I know he's upset with me."

"Honey, he was hurt, and he doesn't deal well with hurt."

"Who does? I didn't deal well with it either."

"When a boy loses his parents, it molds him into the kind of man that doesn't accept loss well. When he left the first time, he felt he wasn't good enough for you, that you were leaving him behind. And now, he thinks you dated him only to dump him. Let him cool off. Give him a call. I'm sure everything will smooth over."

Keri nodded. She *had* dated him only to dump him. But that had only been that first dinner.

Frank's phone rang, and he frowned. "Excuse me." He picked up his cell. "Yep." His frown deepened. "When? Where?" He stood. "Yeah, he's my boy."

Keri saw the alarm on Frank's face and stood as well.

Frank ended the call and looked at Keri. "That was the police." Frank's face darkened, and he drew a breath. "Jaden's car was found crushed on the side of the road. They helicoptered him to Monument Health's trauma center."

A cry escaped Keri's lips. Her hands instinctively flew to her chest, trying to hold herself together.

"I need to go to the hospital," Frank said, already reaching for his keys.

"Is he badly hurt? What happened?" Her voice trembled as she spoke.

"I don't know." He grabbed his jacket.

"I'll take you in my truck, Frank. I'm going with you."

Keri hurried to the hospital, tears flowing and clouding her vision. She sniffed and wiped them away. *Damn it, Jaden.* For a guy who loved cars, he didn't know how to drive.

"He'll be okay," Frank said three times as if repeating a mantra.

Keri nodded and turned into the parking structure at the hospital.

Ben told Jaden to sit down. "Another accident. I don't think anyone is ever going to rent you a car again."

"Where am I?"

Jaden's vision was blurred and hazy. He patted his chest and stomach, sensing wires and machines connected to his body, but there was nothing there. His mouth felt dry and tasted of blood, making his stomach queasy.

"You were in a car accident, Jaden. Unfortunately, it looks like you failed to make that poor girl's Christmas a good one." He checked his tablet. "Though you were doing pretty well, I must say. Until you ran away. Again."

"What are you talking about?" Jaden stood and looked around at the familiar room, feeling less lost. "I've been here before."

"Yes, not too long ago."

"I hit a patch of ice, but it felt like my car was pulled, like someone grabbed it and slammed it against the tree."

Ben nodded. "Yes, your time was up. Or better said, you gave up."

Jaden ran a hand through his hair. He thought hard and then remembered. This weird British guy sent him back after his last accident. "I was supposed to go back and fall in love with Keri? You set that up?"

"Oh no," he said. "I would not do that. You were supposed to make her Christmas happy and memorable. Falling in love with her wasn't necessary."

"But I did. I need to go back and see her."

He shook his head and checked his tablet. "Sit down and relax. We're waiting."

"For what?"

"This is your transition, Jaden. We never said you would get to go back and stay forever. Christmas is special. It's magical. And you got the opportunity to make it special for one lady. Sadly, you didn't finish the task. I was really pulling for you. It will be time to move on soon. Unless a miracle happens."

Jaden wanted to scream, but he narrowed his eyes. "What miracle?"

"Oh, life is full of miracles. Doctors perform them sometimes. Sometimes, others do. We have to wait and see."

Jaden didn't want to *move on*. He wanted to live. With Keri. "Don't I have any say?"

Ben shook his head. "Not anymore."

This seemed so unfair. Going back and making Keri's Christmas special had felt so real. The way she smiled at him over hot cocoa at the ice-skating rink, her laughter as he chased her on the beach, how she'd felt in his arms when they were together in bed and in the shower. "All of that wasn't a dream, was it? I was really with Keri."

"It was real," Ben said.

He focused on Ben's all-knowing eyes. "I have to know what happened after I left. Is Keri okay? Does she think I abandoned her?"

Ben gave him a sympathetic look. "When you left, she was hurt. She didn't understand what had changed and why you suddenly wanted to return to California."

He felt like he swallowed a cotton ball. "I owe it to her to explain. Let me go back, just for a minute. I can't leave her thinking I don't care."

Ben reached out to touch Jaden, but then pulled his hand back. "Your time with Keri was meant to be brief," he said.

"Can I see her? From here."

"You don't want to."

"I do. Please."

Ben considered this, then shrugged, and a big-screen TV appeared. Keri and Uncle Frank were running into a hospital.

Keri and Frank spoke at once. "I'm sorry," she said. "Go ahead."

Frank asked about Jaden, and they told him he was in surgery. He'd had multiple fractures and internal bleeding to organs. His injuries were serious, and they couldn't tell him more yet.

A cry escaped Keri's lips. She shook her head, not wanting to think of Jaden on a surgery table. She fought heart-wrenching sobs that slipped out between choked breaths.

Frank reached out to console her, kissing the side of her head.

"You can go to the waiting area," the nurse said. "We'll let you know when you can see him."

As they walked to the chairs, Keri got control of her emotions. "This is crazy. Where was he going?"

"He just said he had to go think."

He motioned for her to sit down. She sank into a chair and shook her head, covering her face with her hands. The taste of salt from her tears lingered on her lips. "This is all my fault."

"No, it's not. He's the fool who always drives too fast. Damn idiot."

"I love him," Keri said. "I can't lose him again."

Frank placed an arm around her and pulled her close. "The doctors will fix him. He's a fighter."

They sat and waited for hours. Keri texted her mom and told her what had happened. One by one, her parents and her friends arrived to hug Keri and Frank and to wait with them. Five hours later, Jaden was out of surgery and in recovery. They had to wait to see him until the medical crew moved him to a regular room.

Frank was allowed to see Jaden first. Keri waited outside of the room, exhausted and drained of tears. A nurse came with a bag of items they'd taken off Jaden's body when he came in. "Are you a relative?" She asked Keri.

She shook her head. "I'm his . . . I'm his."

Sam walked up. "His uncle is his only relative, and he's inside. Keri is his girlfriend."

"I have a bag of his things. I suppose I can give them to you."

Keri took the plastic bag, and when the nurse left, she looked inside. His wallet. And a burgundy box. With shaking fingers, she pulled it out and opened it, revealing the most beautiful ring she'd ever seen. She lifted her head and exchanged a look with Sam.

Tears filled Keri's eyes again.

Sam put her hand over Keri's and closed the box, returning it to the plastic bag. She wrapped her arms around Keri. "Shh. When he gives you that, you need to act surprised."

"Sam, I can't handle this."

"Marriage does kind of suck, but you can handle it."

Keri half cried and half laughed. "That's not what I mean."

"I know what you mean." She squeezed her tighter. "He'll be fine."

When they let Keri in, and she saw the bruised, deformed man that was on the gurney, she covered her mouth, and even though she didn't think she had any tears left, she cried silently. She sat on a chair beside the bed and gingerly touched his arm. "Oh Jaden, you stupid boy. Why did you go and do this?"

She sat quietly beside him. "You promised you wouldn't leave me again. You promised, and I trusted you. When you get better, we're going to have a fight." She lowered her forehead onto one of his arms. "But first, I'm going to hug and kiss you."

She stayed beside him until they pulled her away. Her parents took her home and gave Frank the keys to Keri's truck so he could go home and sleep.

As soon as she got to her parent's house, Keri passed out, too emotionally drained to stay awake. But she awoke with a start early on Christmas Eve, and her father took her back to the hospital.

She sat by Jaden's bedside all day. Frank did too. He arrived a couple of hours after her. Jaden had not awoken, and he was running a fever. They kept him unconscious because of the swelling to the brain and because of the pain. The doctor checked on him and said the surgery had gone well, but it was too early to say how he'd recover.

In the early evening, Frank went home. But this time, Keri refused to leave. "I'm going to spend Christmas Eve with him," she told the nurse. Since it was a holiday night, the nurse seemed to understand and agreed.

When she left, Keri stared at Jaden. "There's no Christmas without you, Jaden. You're going to heal and be fine, do you hear me? You have a lot of cars to sell to rich people. And the new year is coming, which means new models are coming in, right? Is that how it works? And when you're not selling cars, you need to come and visit Frank and me. I'll visit you too. Maybe I'll even swim naked in your pool after all? Would you like that?"

She touched his hand. "I'll do anything for you, Jaden. It was all real, you know. None of it was fake. There was no game. Not ever. You knew that, didn't you? Did you just get scared and run away from me?" Tears filled her eyes. "It's okay if you did. You can go. I won't keep you. Just don't go *this* way. Go back to California where you can be the sexy guy who drives women crazy and live the life you love so much." She wiped her eyes. "I'm so sorry."

She stood and curled up in a big, cushioned chair. "I'll be right here when you wake up, okay? I'm your best friend, Jade, just like when we were kids." She closed her eyes and fell asleep.

Jaden stared at the screen, unable to look away at the agonizing scene. Ben offered him a remote. "You can rewind and see it again."

Was this guy for real? "I don't want to see it again," he said, frustrated, wanting to slap that remote out of his hand. "I want you to send me back. Let me wake up and talk to her. I'm obviously not dead. Why am I here?"

"You're not dead, yet. That's why you're here. Most likely, you will be soon."

"No! She needs me. You heard her. I can't leave her."

Ben raised an eyebrow. "I told you not to watch. If it makes you feel better, she'll always have a piece of you to love."

Jaden frowned.

"You did give her what she most wanted for Christmas, though the gift will arrive in about nine months. A little less."

Jaden stood, approaching Ben. "Are you telling me she's pregnant?"

Ben nodded. "She sure is. What did you expect after all that sex without a condom?"

Jaden looked around. "Let me out of here. Now!"

"We've been through this. Calm down."

"The woman I love and my future child is down there, and you're going to kill me, and you want me to calm down?"

He reached for Ben and shook him. But suddenly, he couldn't breathe. His hands went to his chest, and he fell to his knees.

CHAPTER
TWENTY-FOUR

J aden started thrashing, his body convulsed violently, his breaths coming in ragged gasps as if he were drowning on dry land. And his face contorted in agony.

Keri, who was half asleep, jumped to her feet. Her voice rose to a frantic scream as she called for help, her words sharp and desperate: "Please, hurry! Something's wrong. He's not breathing!"

Two nurses rushed in, followed by a doctor. "He's having trouble breathing and obviously experiencing chest pain."

Keri was pushed back as three other people ran into the room.

"He has a collapsed lung. I need a needle. Quickly," the doctor said.

Keri stood against the wall, frozen with fear, watching all this as if it were happening far away. The medical staff all talked and worked together as Jaden struggled to breathe. Keri could barely breathe herself. She stumbled out of the room and ran down a long hall where a large window overlooked the hills filled with homes and probably happy people celebrating Christmas Eve.

Keri rested her head on the window. "Please God, please don't take him from me. Give him one more chance. Give *us* one more chance. Look at all the people he's made happy since he's been back: the seniors, my dad, me, even my friends. All he's done over the last three weeks is give selflessly to others. It's his turn now. Give him a long, happy life. It's all I ask, my one Christmas wish."

Getting control of herself, she turned around and pulled the phone from her pocket. "Frank, I'm sorry to wake you. Come down, please. He has a collapsed lung, and they're working on him now."

When she got back to his room, he seemed to be better, no longer struggling. On his side, a syringe was attached to a catheter.

The nurse waved her inside. "He's okay. We're going to leave the catheter in for a few hours to pull out any excess air."

"Why did this happen?"

"From the trauma, broken ribs. He might have had a small puncture. It will heal."

Keri couldn't stop shaking. She hugged her arms tight around herself. "Thank you."

Jaden drew in a deep breath. From where he was on the floor, he looked up at Ben, who spoke to someone, nodded, and made notes on his translucent pad. He smiled at Jaden. "Feeling better?"

Jaden nodded and struggled to his feet. He felt frightened and weak, but he could breathe again.

"The first accident should have killed you. Your body now has the damage from both accidents to heal from, but I have good news."

Feeling emotionally drained, Jaden waited to hear what Ben thought was good news. If it was that he'd finally died and was on his way to Heaven, he didn't want to hear it. He'd already experienced Heaven by Keri's side. Nothing could be better than that.

"You got your Christmas miracle."

His side ached.

"She saved you. She made an excellent case. Though you did run, you gave her the best Christmas season she's ever had. She gets her Christmas wish, and so do you."

Jaden sat back on the floor. He felt terrible. His body started to hurt more and more. "Do I get to go back?"

"You do. You probably won't be back for many years. Have a good life, Jaden. This is really going to hurt."

Jaden moaned and opened his eyes. Keri stood over him, and he closed his eyes again, confused. Where did Ben go? He was about to thank him. Was he back? He couldn't focus or keep his eyes open.

The next time he opened his eyes, his uncle was there too. He remembered hitting that black ice and crashing. He remembered a white room but wasn't sure where it was. And someone was talking to him, a guy who got on his nerves. Damn it, he ached everywhere. Nothing made sense. Machines beeped. His uncle spoke to him, but he couldn't make out what he was saying.

Had Keri been crying? His head pounded, and he wanted everyone and everything gone.

The third time he opened his eyes, he saw Keri sleeping on a chair. A nurse came in. "Are you in pain?"

"Yeah."

"I'll give you a little more painkiller."

"No," Jaden said. He didn't want to sleep again. "What day is it?"

"It's Christmas day. You had a rough night, and scared those who love you. I sent your uncle home, but your girl won't leave." She smiled. "You're going to recover and be good as new soon. Call if you need me."

Jaden closed his eyes but didn't sleep. His girl? Keri didn't even want him? She stirred about an hour later as he watched her sleep.

Her gaze met his, and she straightened. "Hey," she said. "How are you feeling?"

"As bad as I probably look."

She stood and came to his side. "Want me to call the nurse?"

He tried to shake his head, but it hurt to move. "She was here a little while ago. I'm okay. I totaled another car?"

"Yes."

"It's Christmas still?"

"Yes."

"You should be home with your parents."

"I'm exactly where I want to be. You scared me to death."

He closed his eyes. "Go, Keri. I don't want you here."

She looked surprised. "Jaden."

"I'll be fine. When they release me, I'm going back to California where I belong. I shouldn't have bothered you."

"Look at me, Jaden," she said with more force.

His eyelids were heavy, but he did as she asked.

"You get better and do whatever you think is right, but I want you to know this: I love you and I'll be here waiting for you if you ever want me."

He didn't have the energy to respond. Images of her crying or her talking to him filtered through his foggy brain, but he was so confused. And he was coming back to her, wasn't he? He'd made a U-turn before the accident. He'd pleaded with someone to let him come back. A doctor?

She leaned down and dropped a gentle kiss on his lips. "You stole my heart all over again, you stupid boy. I didn't want you to, but you did. I'm yours forever."

Grabbing her purse off the chair, she tossed him one more look, and then she left.

Come back, he wanted to say. *Damn it, I came back for you.*

New Year's Eve was always a fun night. Keri and her friends from high school, plus other friends they made in the last ten years, got together downtown at a hotel to dance all night.

Even though she thought of not going, and her friends told her they completely understood if she didn't show up, Keri decided to go. She'd called the hospital every day, and the nursing staff assured her that Jaden was recovering remarkably well, so well, in fact, that they released him yesterday, and he was back home with his uncle. Even though she wanted to see him and craved being beside him, she needed to give him space and let him leave if he chose to. Having him live and heal was all she cared about.

When her phone rang as she was straightening up her apartment, she saw on the cell phone screen that it was Jaden and was surprised. "Jaden?"

"Hey," he said. "I wanted to talk, so I came to see you. But I can't climb the stairs. Can you come down?"

"Yes, of course. I'll be right down." She told Mochi to stay, and quickly grabbed her jacket and hurried down the stairs, optimistic that this meant they were okay again.

He stood on the sidewalk by himself, looking so much better. The facial swelling had diminished, and his cheeks were a nice red color. Just seeing him standing made her heart surge with gratitude.

"How did you get here?" She looked around for Frank's car.

"I took a Lyft. My uncle said he'd bring me, but I didn't want him waiting in the car for me."

So, they were going to stand out in the cold and talk? "How are you feeling?"

"I'm on heavy drugs, so I'm great." Then he smiled. "I'm kidding. I'm fine."

"You shouldn't be here. You should be resting at home."

"Well, tonight's the New Year's Eve party, and I wondered if I'm still invited."

"Oh Jaden." She shook her head. "I'm sorry about that stupid, insensitive get-even idea. I never seriously considered it."

"No," he said. "Don't be sorry. I've thought a lot about it, and I think you need to go through with it."

Was he trying to hurt her? Tears filled her eyes. "Stop it." She could tell standing in the cold without anything to support his weight was hurting him. "I'm going to get my truck. And I'm taking you home." She parked around the block, so she ran upstairs to get her keys and quickly got the truck, pulling up to the curb beside him. Jaden carefully got inside.

"You got it?"

"Yep."

She helped him put on his seatbelt, trying not to hurt him, then put hers on.

As she drove to his house, she glanced at him at every stop sign. "I want you to get in bed and stay there for at least a week. I'll come to see you every day if you want. I'm a pretty good cook. I can bring dinner for you and your uncle."

"I want to go to the party tonight."

"Why are you being so damned stubborn about this?" She shouted. "You left me when we were supposed to get married. I was beyond heart-broken." She held up her left hand. "You see a ring on this finger? I never got over you."

She stopped at a red light. "Then you stroll back to town and want to insert yourself into my life, giving my father an insanely expensive gift, and you didn't want me to be angry? When the girls said I should get even with you, I laughed. It was stupid. But I considered it for one day. That's why I went out on that first date with you. If I could make you feel just one tiny bit of what I felt, I thought you deserved it."

"I did."

"No, you didn't. Maybe that boy you once were did, but not you now."

The car behind her honked, and she moved forward. "We've gotten to know each other again, and I understand you now. I realize why you left. It hurt me, but it's over, Jaden."

He cleared his throat as if he were going to say something, but he faced away from her, staring out of his window.

"I was never going to dump you," she said quietly, almost as if speaking to herself in that quiet truck. She'd never taken that idea seriously. Mostly, she hadn't wanted her friends to realize how quickly she was falling for him again. "There isn't even an *us* to dump. We're not dating. We're not anything except good friends who had a romantic affair after ten years."

He cursed.

"Don't get mad. You know it's true. And it was wonderful, and I don't regret any of it. And I certainly didn't want it to end." She arrived at Frank's house and parked. "So, if you think I was going to take you to a party to break both our hearts, you're wrong."

"An affair, huh? That's what you think this was?"

She didn't know what *this* was. "You and I have shared so much, Jaden. You've been my love and my friend. We've shared a sweet and innocent past and a passionate, exciting present. This, *you*, are the greatest love of my life.

I just don't see a possible future for us," she admitted. "That's the truth. I wasn't going to say this in public. I wasn't even going to say it to you."

He met her gaze and swallowed. "If you weren't going to dump me and you weren't going to tell me all this, what were you going to do?"

"Love you. Watch you walk away in the new year. Hope you'll come to visit me like you promised. Cherish the moments we shared."

His eyes filled with unshed tears. "You were going to be you, and let me be me."

Nodding, she drew in a shaky breath.

"How very understanding of you."

That sounded like a condemnation. "Thank you."

"Maybe instead you could fight for want you want? You can demand I give you the future that you deserve? You could tell me not to leave?"

Don't leave me she thought and wanted to say those words so badly. But instead, she said, "I shouldn't have to do that. Any man who wants me won't expect me to demand anything. I'm perfectly fine alone. I love you, Jaden, but I won't ever beg you to stay."

He offered a gentle smile. "I keep forgetting who I'm dealing with. Fine, let's get ready for the party."

Her eyes widened. "No."

"I'll show up on my own if you don't take me."

She stared at him, seeing that determination on his face. Not knowing what else to say, she confessed what she'd been holding in, "I was so scared at the hospital, Jaden. I almost lost you. I can live with you going back to California, but I can't live with you dying. You're weak right now. Please stay home and rest."

He reached across and placed a hand over hers on the steering wheel, cringing as if the stretch caused him pain. "Take me to the party."

"I don't want you to end up in the hospital again, Jade. Let's spend the night here with your uncle. The three of us. Please."

But he shook his head.

Now *she* cursed. "If you collapse on me. If you have any complications because of this, I will never talk to you again. I swear." She got out of the car and stomped around the car to open his door. "Let's go get you dressed."

He leaned on her as he got out, and they slowly walked back to the house.

Frank stood when they came in. "I'm glad you brought him back. I told that stubborn mule not to go."

"You should have tied him to his bed. Or maybe he should have stayed at the hospital longer."

"I'm right here. You don't have to talk about me like I'm a kid." Jaden sat on the couch.

"He's insisting on going to the New Year's Eve party."

"He told me." Frank shook his head. "Take good care of him."

Keri placed her hands on her hips. "I'm going to go get dressed. I'll be back in a couple of hours. Do you need help getting dressed?"

"Uncle Frank will help me."

Bending down and touching his bruised face, she kissed his lips. "I don't want to go. I don't understand why you're pushing this."

"I like parties, and I want to see you all dressed up."

Shaking her head, she straightened and left.

CHAPTER TWENTY-FIVE

U ncle Frank helped Jaden dress in his favorite 1818 charcoal gray wool suit that he'd ordered online from his tailor in Los Angeles and had them deliver it overnight. One thing he'd learned over the years was how to dress well. His body ached everywhere, and he still had stitches on his side where he'd damaged his liver and broken ribs.

After tonight, he'd do what Keri suggested and stay in bed for a week or two, or at least inside this house.

"You know, she didn't leave your side the whole time you were in critical condition at the hospital."

Jaden nodded and attached his bowtie. "Yep."

"I don't think I ever had a woman love me like she loves you."

Jaden placed a hand on his uncle's shoulder. "They would have, but they all knew you were a man hoe."

"A what?"

Jaden chuckled. "You never let anyone get close."

"I guess. I enjoy my freedom and have had too much fun to give it up. But this girl is exactly what you need."

"What about what she needs?"

Uncle Frank stood back. "You look like every woman's dream. A little beat up, but a great catch. You know what she needs."

They went to the living room and waited for Keri to show up, and when she did, Jaden was speechless. She looked gorgeous in a long, sparkly gray dress that clung to the curves of her body that he now knew so well.

"Wow," she said.

"That's what I was thinking," he said.

"You look like a million bucks," Uncle Frank said, kissing Keri's cheek.

"Thank you."

After saying goodbye to his uncle, they carefully walked to her truck.

"So, tell me about this party."

"After high school, we all decided to meet once a year at New Year and have a big celebration, so we didn't lose touch with each other. We used to pick someone's house, but after everyone started getting married and made new friends, it got too big, so now we rent a hotel conference room and pay for catering, hire a DJ and . . . it's really fun."

"Sounds like it. I'm kind of nervous to see people I haven't seen since high school. I didn't come to the ten-year reunion last summer."

"No one expected you to. Or at least, I didn't."

Of course, she didn't. Who really attended those things? Apparently, his high school class did if they got together every year.

When they arrived at the grand entrance of the Alex Johnson Hotel, Jaden's eyes widened at the sea of people milling about. How big was this thing? But as they entered the lobby, everyone seemed to be going in different directions. The hotel had its own New Year's Eve celebration in the ballroom where the sounds of music and laughter filtered into the lobby.

"We have the Lincoln room. This way," Keri said.

As they walked in, people started waving at Keri immediately. Clearly, she'd kept in touch with everyone and was one popular lady. He recognized a few people and even saw a couple of guys he'd been good friends with during high school.

"Whoa, Jaden, this is a surprise, man," said his friend Jared. Teachers used to call them the two "J"s.

Keri jumped in front of Jared just as he was going to hug Jaden. "Don't touch him. He was in a bad accident, and he's healing."

Jared laughed. "You've got your own bodyguard, huh? Definitely seems like old times."

Jaden and Jared shook hands gently. Jared introduced his wife, who had also gone to their high school.

Sam and the rest of Keri's gang had a table reserved for them, so Jaden and Keri joined them.

"Hi Jaden," Sam said, dropping a kiss on his cheek. "Are you feeling better?"

He nodded. She'd come to see him at the hospital after he'd thrown Keri out. He'd been so confused when he'd woken up in the hospital. He remembered feeling and being hurt and angry with Keri. But he also had this weird memory of hearing her talk to him, of watching her cry. Maybe unconscious people could really hear those around them.

At the hospital, Sam had confessed that the idea of Keri getting close to him in order to dump him had been all hers. "She flat out told me that she wasn't going to go through with the plan. Many times. The last time was when we went Christmas shopping together, well before she followed you to California."

"Whatever. It doesn't matter anymore," Jaden had said, wanting her and all of them to go away. He felt like hell. He'd had two accidents three weeks apart, and his body and head throbbed.

"I hope that's not true because she cares about you. You know Keri, she never intended to deliberately hurt you."

But she had. Just the thought that she'd been acting and faking her interest in him had cut through his soul. "Okay. Thanks," he'd said.

"I hope you get better soon, Jaden. You scared all of us. We all want you back in our lives."

Now, as they took a seat at the round table, her three friends with their husbands, who all talked at once, Jaden felt lucky to be included and was happy that he'd forced Keri to bring him.

As the evening progressed and everyone ate dinner, couples danced to music from their high school days, plus some modern hits, and mingled around the room, Jaden enjoyed watching since he couldn't participate.

"Let me know when you want to leave," Keri leaned close to him a couple of hours after they arrived.

"I want to stay until after midnight."

"You're not in pain?"

"A little," he admitted. "But I'm happy to be here sitting beside you."

She cupped his face and dropped a gentle kiss on his lips. "I'm happy, too."

When it got close to midnight, he decided it was time. So, he stood and headed to the stage while Keri was away from the table, laughing and socializing with people he didn't recognize.

He carefully climbed the stage and spoke with the DJ, who nodded and, after the song finished, told the crowd that Jaden had a few words to say to the group.

The room went silent, and he saw Keri's shocked and almost panicked expression.

He took the microphone. "The music and festivities will start back up in a second. Sorry to interrupt everyone's fun, but I haven't seen you all in ten years, and it's been really nice to reconnect with you again tonight."

People clapped.

"Meeting your spouses and finding out all the great things you've been up to has been super cool. But that's not why I wanted to come tonight."

He glanced at Keri. "I left ten years ago, suddenly. I was supposed to marry a beautiful, sweet girl, and I just left."

She shook her head as if to say, 'don't do this,' but he kept going.

"I broke her heart. Some of you know that and hated me for it. I don't blame you and can't give you a good reason for what I did. The truth is that I got an opportunity to leave, to get out of here where I felt I didn't have a future. I got a great job offer, and I took it. I thought there would always be other girls, but maybe not other job opportunities. When I told my uncle my idea, he told me not to hesitate. To leave. So, I did."

Keri's eyes were glassy now, and she was starting to look angry.

"My uncle wasn't always the best role model, especially with women. He loves Keri. Don't hold that against him, Keri. It was all me. But I want to say tonight that I'm sorry. When I got back, she didn't want to even talk to me, but because she has a huge heart and a forgiving soul, she eventually did."

The room was completely silent. Distant music from the ballroom was the only sound, that and his voice.

He gazed at Keri. "I want to say here, in front of everyone, that I was a heartless jerk. I don't deserve her. I was wrong about there always being other girls. No one captured my heart like she did." As difficult and painful as it was, he struggled to get down on one knee. He heard Keri gasp and scream 'no,' running to climb up on stage.

"Oh, good. This is a lot easier with you close. Keri, I was going to propose on Christmas Eve in front of your parents, but I ran away again. Just the thought of you not really wanting me infuriated me. I'm a fool, but I love you. I want you to marry me, and I'm asking here in front of all your friends."

"Jaden."

"Wait a minute. And I'm okay if you say no. I won't run. I'll keep asking you. Again and again. Until I prove to you that I'm not leaving you ever again. Go ahead, say no."

Tears wet her cheeks as she looked at him.

He took a ring out of his pocket and held it up to her. "But if it's a yes, I'd like to place this ring on your finger."

She didn't make a move or say anything. Her head slowly started to shake, and his heart sank just a little, but he understood.

"The plan was to turn you down tonight," she said. "Though I never expected a proposal."

People in the audience gasped, and Sam cried out, "Are you crazy?"

Keri looked out at her friends as if just remembering they were there.

"I don't think I can stay down on my knee much longer," Jaden said.

"Oh, I'm sorry." Keri helped him to his feet. "I can't believe you did this," she whispered.

"I want to declare to the whole world that I love you."

She gave him her left hand. "Didn't you tell me that, technically, we're still engaged?"

"That we are. But I'd still like to hear a yes."

"Yes," she screamed. Everyone in the room started to clap and cheer, and the DJ played Al Green's "Let's Stay Together."

Jaden held out a hand, and they danced slowly, very slowly, on the stage. Everyone else took to the dance floor below.

"This is why you wanted to come tonight?" She looked at and caressed his bruised but still handsome face.

"You deserved the public apology and the public proposal."

"All I ever wanted was you. How are we going to make this work? I don't want to move, even though your house is fabulous."

"It's just an empty house with no one who loves me. I'll live wherever you want."

"Let's get off this stage and get you home."

"After midnight. It's only a few more minutes."

So, as the countdown started, they rang in the new year together, with their friends' congratulations.

CHAPTER TWENTY-SIX

K eri sat on the cold gyno table in her gynecologist's office, waiting to confirm the result she already knew. She'd taken an at-home pregnancy test twice, and both times, it had come back positive. She wanted an official confirmation and to cancel her future insemination appointments.

When Doctor Pruitt entered the room with a big smile, Keri released a breath she'd been holding. "I'm pregnant?"

"Congratulations. I can't believe it happened so fast. I have to tell you that it rarely takes the first time. I guess you got a Christmas miracle."

It seemed like her life was full of miracles lately. "So, what now?"

"Now, we keep an eye on you and schedule regular visits to check on the baby's growth. I want you to take some vitamins and enjoy being pregnant."

Keri couldn't be more excited. She was finally going to be a mom, and the first person she wanted to tell was Sam. Under normal circumstances, she'd want to share it with Jaden, but how would she tell the man who'd recently proposed to her that she was going to have an anonymous donor's baby?

She dialed Sam's number, hoping for a chance to drop by her house.

"I'm picking the twins up from school and taking them to scouts. Let's meet for coffee at the Starbucks off Mount Rushmore Road, which is close to where I'm dropping them off."

"Okay." The city was recovering from the holidays, but Christmas decorations were still everywhere. Keri didn't mind. She loved extending the holidays by a couple of weeks. The snow had melted away, and though it was still cold, it was much easier to get around. No doubt January would bring another storm soon, so she was grateful for the clear roads. She parked, went inside, and ordered lattes for her and Sam.

A few minutes later, Samantha strolled in, looking only mildly frazzled. "Thank you! I needed this. It's been a long day. I'm so grateful to the scout leader. They're working on designing their derby cars or whatever they are."

"Jaden would love that. You should have him help the boys."

"Patrick helps, but he tends to want to build the car for them. Is Jaden back?"

Keri shook her head. He'd stayed in town a week after New Year's Day to heal and see his doctor, then flew back to California for work. She was going to spend the rest of the month with him in California after her own doctor's appointment. "He's coming back next month to look for a headquarters out here to run his business. Eduardo is going to run things in California. But I have other news to share with you."

Sam sipped her latte with a satisfied moan. "What? You chose your wedding date?"

"I'm pregnant."

Sam choked on her hot drink and put the cup down. "Crap, you'd better schedule that wedding now."

Keri played with the coffee stir. "Sam, I don't know if it's Jaden's baby."

This time, Sam laughed. "Good one. It's not April Fool's Day yet."

"I'm serious."

"Who else's could it be? I haven't seen you dating anyone in what? Nine months? A year? As much as I tried to set you up with great guys, you wouldn't go out with anyone."

"I decided recently that I wanted to have a baby. And I didn't want to wait to meet someone. So, I ordered sperm from a sperm bank, and—."

"What?!" Those seated close by turned to look at them. "Why would you do something like that? And why is this the first time I'm hearing about this?"

"I didn't want to say anything until I knew it was successful."

Sam leaned in. "You *used* the sperm?"

"Well, of course. What do you think I did? Bought it just to have it in my house?"

"Wait, wait." She placed a hand on Keri's arm. "This . . . stuff was delivered to your house?"

"Yes, and I took it to my gynecologist and had the procedure done."

"Oh my God, Keri." She shook her head. And leaned back in her chair. "I can't believe you did this. How many times?"

"Just once. That's the thing. And it was right before Jaden and I, you know, got together."

"So, now you don't know who got you pregnant."

"Right. At least not yet. But I don't know what to say to Jaden."

"Shit," Sam said. "He's going to freak out. Don't let him drive a car."

Keri laughed. "He knows about the insemination, but I still don't know when exactly I got pregnant."

"Wait, he knows?"

"I told him. In fact, he carried the tank into my apartment for me when it arrived."

"You told *him*, but not me. Now, I'm pissed."

Keri smiled. "I told him because he happened to be there when it arrived. And back then, I just wanted him to go away." Growing serious, she said. "But I still don't know how to break it to him that I'm pregnant."

"I guess you just tell him."

"When we had sex without a condom, he knew I could get pregnant. He doesn't really want to be a dad, but he was okay with risking it."

"Then he's an idiot. He should have gotten a condom."

"The first time, we didn't have one and..." She felt her face warm. "Stopping wasn't an option."

"Oh, brother." Sam rolled her eyes.

"After that." She sighed, unable to say what was in Jaden's mind. "He knew I wanted a baby."

"Well, that's sweet, but you're both idiots. It's a baby—a lifelong commitment. You don't agree to "give" someone a baby. Sounds like he was well-informed. Now, he gets to be a dad."

"What if the baby is not his?"

Sam stared at Keri and shook her head as if to tell her she'd made a dumbass decision and would have to live with the consequences. "It's a little late to think about that now. When are you going to see him?"

"Mochi and I are driving to California tomorrow."

"Good, don't sit here and worry about it anymore. Go tell him."

But Keri did worry. Jaden waited for her at his home and opened the door with a big grin, like he hadn't seen her in months. He pulled her into his arms and scratched Mochi behind the ears.

"I'll show him the backyard and let him smell around and scent every damned tree," Jaden said. When he walked back inside, he eagerly shared every detail of the extensive preparations he had been making to entrust Eduardo with the operation of his business in California. "I'll still have to fly out every month or so and probably travel to other states as well, depending on who my client is. But I'll be able to work from Rapid City most of the time. Next month, I'll search for and find a place there. Mostly, I'll need a suitable office. The cars will stay in Los Angeles."

Grateful to let him do all the talking, Keri listened.

"Have a seat at the dining table," he said. "I ordered some food. They delivered it about thirty minutes ago, but it's still warm." He opened a bottle of wine.

"Oh, no thank you."

"Come on. Let's celebrate."

She took the bottle out of his hands, placed it on the table, and gripped his hands. "How are you doing?"

"Great. Not one hundred percent yet, but good."

"I'm glad. Jaden, I have to tell you something."

"Why so serious?"

"Because I don't know how you're going to feel about what I need to tell you."

"What is it?" He frowned.

"I saw my doctor, and I'm pregnant."

His eyes widened. "Wow. I was going to ask how your appointment went, but I figured it was a no since you didn't call full of excitement." He leaned across and dropped a kiss on her lips. "Well, congratulations. Is that what you're supposed to say to moms-to-be?" He laughed, squeezed her hands, and reached for a pitcher of water.

"I don't know what you're supposed to say."

"Why don't you look happy? Isn't this what you wanted?" He poured water into her glass and wine into his own.

"I'm thrilled. I'm unbelievably happy. But, Jaden, you know I had an insemination done before we got together. I don't know whose baby this is."

"Ah." He nodded and scooted his chair beside hers. He pulled her in close and wrapped an arm around her. "Is that what you're worried about?" Leaning his head to the side, he softly kissed her jaw, then her lips. "This is *our* baby."

Keri released her breath. "You're sure you feel that way? You won't wonder if it's really yours?"

"First of all, it won't matter. And secondly, I know it's mine. I feel it. I don't know why, but I just know it has to be."

"Have I told you that I love you?" Keri said, cupping his face.

"You might have to remind me how much."

"I will," she promised. "Every day."

"Thank you for waiting for me to grow up and come to my senses."

"You were worth the wait."

He took her lips in a deep kiss, then stood and bent down to lift her out of her chair, but quickly put her down. "Ouch, I forgot, I can't do that."

"Oh baby." She caressed his side. "I'm starving anyway. Let's eat first."

He sat beside her again to eat delicious Lebanese food: hummus with pita, falafel wraps, rice pilaf, and kafta, which were chicken meatballs filled with spices, onions, parsley, and breadcrumbs.

Mochi scratched at the sliding glass door. "I'll let him back in," Jaden said. He led Mochi to the kitchen and put down a bowl of water, which the dog nearly emptied.

"When do we get to talk about names?" Jaden returned to the table.

"If it's a girl, how about Elisabeth?"

"My mom's name?"

For dessert, they had baklava. Keri pulled a sticky square and took a bite. She nodded. "Your uncle talked a lot about her when we were in the hospital waiting for you to come out of your coma."

"Hmm. Well, maybe. I like that name. And if it's a boy?"

"Not sure. What do you think?"

"How about Ben?"

"Ben? Why?"

He thought about it for a second. Had a nice ring, but...naw. "On second thought, maybe not."

She licked her fingers. "Benjamin. I kind of like that. Has an intelligent air to it. But we have a lot of time to think about it."

As they continued to enjoy more baklava, wine, and water, they planned more of their brilliant future together, and Keri knew that when they looked back, they would only remember this first magical Christmas they'd had together and the days that followed, not all the years that came before.

Jaden woke up around three in the morning and couldn't fall back asleep. Maybe he'd eaten too much. Maybe it was the mind-blowing sex. Maybe he just had too much on his mind. He was going to be a husband and a father. Holy shit. Opening the living room sliding glass door, he slipped outside and sat by his pool. Mochi followed him out and ran around, looking for a place to do his business.

A slight breeze moved the palm tree fronds, and Jaden gazed up at the few stars that were visible. Unlike out in South Dakota, you didn't get to see as many stars here. But it was still a gorgeous night. The practically cloudless, dark, velvety sky made him feel a peaceful and weird connection to the universe. He felt small and large at the same time.

Jaden wasn't religious, but his heart was so complete that, for some reason, he said, "Hey, God. Thanks."

No booming voice came down from heaven, but he felt like someone had whispered *well done* into his soul.

He nodded. "Yep, I think I finally got it right."

He stood. "Come on, Mochi. Let's go back inside."

Mochi happily bounced back to Jaden's side. He patted Mochi's furry head and together, they climbed the stairs. Mochi curled up in his bed that Keri had lugged all the way from South Dakota, and Jaden slid back into bed with the love of his life.

She moaned and wrapped an arm around his shoulder. Pulling her near, he closed his eyes and went happily to sleep, holding his two Christmas miracles in his arms.

The End

Let Us Begin

Julia's 2023 Women's Fiction title

D id you love *Christmas Without You*? Then you should read *Let Us Begin* a Women's Fiction novel by Julia Amante!

Reinvention and redemption: One immigrant's struggle for a better life.

Salvador arrives in the United States from Argentina with one big, unfocused goal, to become successful at something. He knows that America is the land of opportunity, and if he works hard, he will triumph.

Together with his childhood sweetheart, he settles in the Big Apple where dreams come true. But this ambitious young immigrant soon learns that it takes more than hard work and charisma to succeed and is changed by the harsh realities of living in New York.

Everyone has advice for Salvador as he moves from one dead-end job to another, attempting to reinvent himself. But the best advice comes from the loving letters he gets from his father. They keep him grounded and remind him of the man he wants to be until he loses this moral compass the day his father succumbs to diabetes.

As the 1960s roll into the 1970s and America and Salvador become less innocent, he finds himself in California where he starts his own business, and it finally looks like the American Dream is within his grasp.

But things get complicated when Argentina is involved in a war in the early 1980s, and Salvador must decide where his allegiances lie. One wrong decision and bold act can bring his dreams crumbling down, and Salvador soon realizes that there are consequences for being impulsive and disloyal.

In the end, Salvador learns that there are boundaries men should not cross and that the love of family is perhaps the only worthwhile dream Americans should pursue. Spanning decades, *Let Us Begin* is a moving story filled with joy and despair about a family searching for a home and a place to belong.

Read the first two chapters below.

CHAPTER ONE

The year was 1964 and life was good in Argentina. The 1950s, said to be the golden decade of abundance and overall well-being, bled into the early '60s, and it was especially good for my family. My parents owned a pizzeria bar frequented by neighbors. Every night started slowly and became a festive celebration by evening as music from Palito Ortega, Leo Dan, and of course, The Beatles played in the background, and beer and wine flowed. The salon had about twenty tables which were rarely open for long.

All through high school, my brother Theodoro and I helped by busing the tables and taking food orders. You never knew who would stop by, so most of the time, work felt more like hanging out with friends and family.

That year, I was about to make a decision that would change all our lives and my future forever, and I made it because I believed in the promise of a man I had never met. An American President who challenged the world to dream in his inaugural address in 1961. I was only 19 years old when I listened to his words about what we could all do worldwide to fight for the "freedom of man" and liberty. Every word he said was magic to my ears. The challenge he said, was for our generation, *my generation*. I had been enchanted.

It wasn't until three years later, as I bussed the table of some friends of my parents—friends who had just returned from a trip to the United States—that I considered accepting that challenge.

"What's it like?" I asked the couple and took a seat beside my parents to hear about the grand country to the north.

"Everything you imagine and more," Mr. Martinez said. "It's a place where you envision what you want, and it appears before you." He slapped his hands together and spread out his fingers.

We all laughed.

But Kennedy's words came back to me, "Together let us explore the stars, conquer the deserts, eradicate disease, tap the ocean depths and encourage the arts and commerce." *Of course*, all was possible in America. The word "limits" didn't exist in their vocabulary.

"For a young man like you, there's nothing you can't achieve. There's work everywhere. Don't waste your life here. Go there and become someone great."

I listened with rapt attention and nodded. My mother told me to stop asking questions and take care of the other customers, so I stood and moved away, but I kept coming back, wanting to know more. I went to sleep that night excited and filled with the dreams only a twenty-two-year-old can have.

In my half-asleep, half-awake state, I saw a light blue sky full of clouds that formed various shapes before dissolving into nothing, then reforming into something new. Was I asleep or was I dreaming? I didn't know.

But dreams are like clouds, aren't they? You see them, almost feel like you can touch them, that they're real. But as the wind begins to blow, they fade away, change, transform into something ill-defined and vague. You realize at that moment that the pictures were never real at all. That dreams are just illusions that fool you into trusting and believing in them, leaving you feeling absurd.

I frowned, rubbing my eyes with the heels of my palms, and stretched, forcing myself to wake up.

I had dreams all right, and I was going to make them all come true. I was as sure of that as I was of the breath in my lungs. I didn't have any doubts. My whole life was stretched out ahead of me, and I was ready for it all.

"Salvador, Salvador, get up," my mother's voice pushed my thoughts away. I opened my eyes and reached for my glasses on the nightstand. My mother was on the other side of the closed door of my tiny room that barely had enough space for my Mahogany bedroom set that included, the nightstand and an armoire. The room had no windows.

"*Sí, Mamá*, I'm awake," I called out.

"You're going to be late for classes."

"No, no, I'm up." I kicked my legs out of my twin bed and stood, scratching the back of my head. Quickly, I flipped on the lights and pulled a pair of pants out of the armoire and a button-up shirt. I went to the bathroom down the hall to wash my face, brush my teeth, and comb my hair. I grabbed my wallet and keys and strolled out of the apartment we owned behind our pizzeria bar.

Mamá worked tirelessly from morning to night, ensuring the restaurant ran like clockwork. Up before dawn, she prepared the pizza dough, cut and sliced the ingredients for the pizza, and placed them in their refrigerated slots. She kept everything in the kitchen spotless, from the appliances to the tables to the floor. I teased her that she could run a military regiment with her discipline and sense of organization.

Papá hired the employees which he hadn't needed to do lately. He ordered the ingredients, handled the finances, and took care of the back end of the business. He'd been diagnosed with diabetes and often wasn't well. We all relied on *Mamá* too much, but she never complained.

Together, they made a good team.

"Ah, finally, the king gets up," *Papá* said as I entered the restaurant, grabbed a quick cup of coffee, and drank it while standing.

I grinned, kissed my father good morning on both cheeks, downed the last gulp of coffee, and hurried past my *viejo,* who stood at the counter. "I'm late," I told him

"You don't say."

"I had a late night." I'd gone out after things slowed down at the restaurant, too excited with thoughts of my future swirling around in my head.

"An irresponsible man is never rewarded, Salvador. I expect you to help tonight. Remember that."

"I will."

"We can't afford to hire more help."

"I know, I know." I didn't have to be told that they were struggling. I knew that. Before *Papá* got sick, he'd been a journalist and then worked for an insurance agency making good money. My parents had saved enough to buy the restaurant and were doing well, but now they had to rely only on the profits from the pizzeria to pay for everything, and things were tight. "You can count on me. *Chau, Viejo.*" I was almost at the front door, ready to escape before *Papá* couldremind me that usually, they couldn't count on me, but I ran back in and kissed my mother. "*Chau, Vieja. Te quiero mucho.*"

She beamed and patted my cheek. "*Mi hijo querido,*" she said. "*Te quiero mucho, tambien.*"

I ran out, jumped on the motorbike that my father bought me last year, and sped off, honking at the cars on my way out. Damn cars will run you over if you don't warn them. Stop signs were only suggestions to most Argentine drivers.

I hurried to downtown Rosario, not to the school of engineering where my class had started fifteen minutes ago. I had no interest in taking classes. Yes, I was doing well, and sure, the classes were interesting, but the world didn't need another chemical engineer. And I didn't need to become one more overworked engineer making a big company rich. Instead, I'd asked Luisa to meet me by the river, and as I pulled my motorbike into the parking lot, I saw my elegant, thin, always perfectly dressed girlfriend sitting on a bench, waiting for me.

I jumped off the bike, pulled out my cigarettes, shook one loose and lit it. I strolled toward her, happy and excited to share the biggest decision of my life. When I reached the bench, I placed a foot on the seat beside her, rested my elbow on my knee, and leaned close to her. "Hey, beautiful," I said. "Mind if I join you?"

"Salvador." She smiled. "I thought you forgot that you told me to meet you here. Or that I had the wrong day. What are we doing here anyway?"

I took another drag of the cigarette and put it out, blowing smoke away from her, then reached for her hand. "Let's walk."

The first time I'd seen Luisa, I had been only fifteen. On New Year's Eve, she came to the restaurant to dance, literally walking into my life. My parents closed the restaurant after ten, and we partied all night. I thought she was cute in her bright red dress with no defined waistline and crazy high-heeled shoes, but she didn't pay any attention to me. She danced with older boys or stayed shyly beside her sisters. But, she continued to show up every New Year's Eve with her sisters, whom I came to learn were related to my neighbor. Each year, she looked sexier, her dresses got shorter and shapelier. Her short brown hair grew a little longer until it finally touched her shoulders and curled around her ears. Finally, when I turned eighteen, I asked her to dance. She'd said yes, and we'd been going out ever since.

She took my hand, and we walked along the paved path beside the Paraná River that crossed the city of Rosario where I'd spent many happy summers with friends. No breeze blew today, and the dark chocolate river water moved almost lazily.

"So, I have something important to tell you, to ask you."

"Okay," she said, sounding unsure.

"I'm going to move to America, to the United States," I blurted out and wished I'd said it differently, but I couldn't keep it inside anymore.

She looked momentarily shocked but recovered with a couple of blinks of her caramel eyes. She continued to walk beside me but pulled her thin hand out of mine and brushed some of her shoulder-length hair back. "Really? When?"

"Soon, I don't know."

"What about your school, getting your degree? Your parents —"

"The hell with the degree. What's that going to get me? My *viejos* are struggling at the restaurant. They're supporting my brother until he gets his law degree. They're supporting me, and I don't want them to do that anymore. I'm twenty-two. I'm a man and still living with my parents." Not that living with my parents was so out of the ordinary. Everyone usually lived in their family home until they got married, but that wasn't what I wanted anymore.

"Listen." I stopped walking and took both her hands. "I can go there for a few years. Make money. Then I can come back, and we can get married and have a great life together."

Luisa nodded, still looking like she didn't believe me, like she was sure that if I left, she'd never see me again. "Married?" she asked.

I grinned with a cocky smile because I was kind of sure of her answer. "Yes, you want to marry me someday, don't you?"

"I don't know. You never asked."

"I'm asking, Luisita. I don't have a ring right now, but I want you to marry me. What do you say?"

A smile grew on her lips. "Okay," she said.

"Okay? How about yes? Yes, yes I want to marry you because I love you."

She laughed. "Yes, yes, yes, I want to marry you."

I pulled her tight against my body, hugging her and not wanting to let her go. Leaving her would be the only bad part about moving to the U.S. With heels, Luisa was the same height as me. At five-foot-seven, I was not a tall man. But today, she wore simple sandals, so her head rested on my shoulder. I picked her up and twirled her around. When I stopped, we both laughed, and I kissed her.

"I do love you," she said.

"We're going to have a wonderful life," I promised because why wouldn't we? We were young and in love, and I planned to create a great life for us. "Remember President Kennedy's inauguration speech?"

She shook her head, a confused frown creating a wrinkle between her eyebrows.

"He said it was up to our generation to build the future. That whether we are an American citizen or a citizen of the world, we can all work together to create a better world." I retook her hand and walked away from the river. "Before the bastards killed him last year, he had a vision and goals that were good, Luisita. And I do too. I want to live in the greatest country in the world. I want to be part of Kennedy's vision and know I can be."

I looked across the park where the National Monument to the Argentine flag stood proudly. The majestic monument, shaped like a giant ship about to enter the river, seemed to question my words defiantly. The gorgeous monument filled me with pride. I loved my country, of course. Argentina *was* a great and proud country, but only a baby compared to America. There was no comparison. "And when I come back, I want to work to better our country, too," I said, almost as an apology to my own nation. But I wouldn't feel guilty about following my heart.

"Aren't you scared to go to a foreign place? You don't speak the language and don't know what it's like."

"I can speak some English. My parents' friends were visiting the restaurant last night, and they have family members living in New York. They said that it's ridiculously easy to get a job. Everyone is hiring, and they pay a lot. I can make a couple hundred dollars a week. Do you know how amazing that is? My parents won't have to support me anymore."

"Have you told them?"

"Not yet." I didn't know how they would take it. "I think I have enough saved from working at the pizzeria to get my airline ticket." My parents didn't actually pay me. They just told me to get what I needed from the register. I put a little away each week, whatever I didn't spend on Luisa or cigarettes.

The lids of her eyes lowered, and the corners of her lips dipped for a moment before she flashed a soft smile. "I'm excited for you."

"For us. Be excited for us. I'll write you every day."

She shook her head, knowing me better than that.

"Okay, every week. And when I come back, we'll start our life together."

CHAPTER TWO

October 17, 1964

My Dearest Parents,

I write this first letter on Lan Chile stationary to share that the trip to New York has been a success. They sat me in a seat where I could see the takeoff and landing perfectly. We dined using excellent silverware. We had two stops in Chile and Panama before we landed in Miami. Miami appears to be a pleasant city though I can't tell you much because I was only there a couple of hours—two hours and forty minutes to be exact—before I caught a Greyhound to New York. A Greyhound is a large bus. We passed through Washington D.C. Washington has an Obelisk just like the one in Buenos Aires which makes sense since they are both two grand capitals. I saw the White House also! The road that the bus took gave us a perfect view.

I will share nothing about New York for now. It's too impressive for words, but I will share more in future letters.

I'd like to tell you that Pepa's sister and her husband welcomed me into their home as if I were their son. When I arrived, they made me feel very comfortable.

Well, I believe my pen has run out of ink. I blame the pen for ending this letter so quickly. My hope is that you feel the love I send through these words, and I await your response, filled no doubt, with your love back.

Your Son,

Salvador

Finding a job in New York wasn't difficult. Pedro Llonch, the friend of my parents who agreed to let me stay with them, had connections. One of his friends, Raul worked at a fabulous steakhouse and seafood restaurant in downtown Manhattan. They needed a cook, and I had two hands, a brain, and had watched my mother cook all my life. That made me qualified both in Pedro's and my opinion. I dressed in the one suit I had brought with me, slicked my hair back, put on a little cologne, shined my dress shoes, and went for the interview.

The tables were already half full at six in the evening, and people waited to be seated.

"For how many?" the man at the door asked.

"Excuse me?" I asked. I had been practicing my English, but honestly, it was going to take me a while to learn to speak well and to understand.

"How many in your party?" he asked again.

"I interview," I said. And when the host frowned, I added, "I new cook."

"Oh," he said, looking at my clothes as if still confused. "Sure. The kitchen's that way. Stay to your left and go down the first hallway. The office is the second door on the right."

"Thank you," I said, not quite sure what he'd said, but he pointed, and I headed in that direction.

When I got to the back, I looked into an office where a pretty blonde sat at a desk. She smiled. "Sir, are you looking for the bathroom?"

"I new cook," I repeated. "Speak to Raul? Interview, please."

"Interview?" She stood. "Just a minute." She disappeared for a few seconds and returned with an older man who introduced himself as Carlos.

Carlos dressed in a nice suit like mine and eyed me curiously as he held out his hand. I shook it and tried to explain again why I was there. I stated that Raul, one of his waiters, had mentioned they needed a new cook.

"Yes, yes, you're Raul's friend?" Thankfully, he spoke Spanish, and as soon as he started talking and I heard his accent, I realized he was a Spaniard.

"Not exactly. Raul is a friend of a friend, but I want to say that my parents own a restaurant in Argentina," I explained in Spanish. "It's a pizzeria, of course, nothing fancy like this, but I helped out all the time. I know a lot about running a restaurant. And I'm quick to learn."

He patted my shoulder. "Young man. I need a cook. You can leave the running of the restaurant to me. I can pair you up with the chef if you're willing to learn, and if you will show up to work on time every night, you've got the job."

"Absolutely. You can count on me."

"Then you're hired. Get out of those clothes, grab an apron, and go to the kitchen."

I looked down at my suit. "This is all I have with me today."

He motioned for me to follow him. In the back, he threw a pair of jeans and a T-shirt at me. "Change. Meet me in the kitchen."

And that was how it started.

The kitchen was a busy place, and I was introduced to a Gallego who was the main chef. He looked me over like he wasn't impressed, frowning at my baggy jeans and dress shoes. I didn't blame him; I felt foolish.

"Stand here," he said, pointing to a corner of an extraordinary island with burners on both ends and a food preparation area in the center. Behind us was more room to prepare food and a sink.

He handed me a crate of vegetables. "Wash these."

I nodded and took them to the sink to scrub carrots, potatoes, celery, and other vegetables. He showed me how to cut and steam the carrots. Some potatoes were set aside for baking while others were roasted with chicken, and others for mashed potatoes.

I spent the first week learning my way around the kitchen, being no more than an errand boy and jumping every time the chef needed something. When I asked his name, he said I could call him Chef.

By the second week, he started teaching me how to make a few dishes. I came in before the evening diners arrived, and I worked with him and another cook, a Puerto Rican named Javier, who had been there a month longer than I had. The Spaniard Chef was strict but an amazing cook. Over the next weeks, I learned to make Paella Valenciana, *tortillas de papa* which were potato omelets similar to the ones my mom made in Argentina. I also learned the perfect way to cook lobster, how to grill steaks to perfection, and to make various delicious tapas.

The atmosphere and constant activity challenged me, but it was fun. I learned that this upscale restaurant in Manhattan had a good reputation where people with money dined before and after going to Broadway plays.

Being in New York, in the buzz and thrill of the city, energized me so much that I didn't sleep for hours when I got home.

Of course, the hot work in the kitchen could get exhausting; I hadn't worked this hard my entire life, but the Spanish owner, Carlos paid well. He came to stand beside me when I escaped outside, smoking a cigarette one night. I thought he was going to yell at me, but he said, "You're a good worker, Salvador. And you're smart. Chef Hugo is impressed with you, and he's not easily impressed."

Ah, so his name was Hugo. I nodded my appreciation. "Thank you, sir."

"Do you like the job?"

Did I? I did. Time went by fast. I made good money. "I appreciate the opportunity," I said.

"But do you like cooking?"

"Sure."

"Maybe you should consider going to culinary school. You're talented. I could see you becoming a great chef someday."

I laughed. "I don't think so."

"Think about it, Salvador. Think big. I don't know what you're doing in this country, but you're well educated, polite, clean, and you can go far if you use your intelligence well." The Spaniard disappeared back inside, and I put my cigarette out. The freezing night air penetrated my clothes so that I couldn't stand outside for too long.

I intended to go far, but I wasn't going to become a chef and work at a restaurant for the rest of my life. I saw how hard my parents worked, how they were slaves to a restaurant, and never had a night off. They worked, worked, worked.

No, thank you. I'd stay here for a while, but I had bigger plans. I wasn't sure what yet, but someday soon, it would come to me. I felt it in my bones, those that weren't frozen.

When I got home that night at almost 2AM to the little room the Llonch couple offered me, I lay back in bed and pulled out the photo of Luisa and me, dressed up for her sister's wedding. We looked perfect together. My heart picked up speed when I thought of Luisa. I didn't want to live without her for the next year or longer.

I could see now that it would take some time to earn enough money to return home to Argentina. I wanted to have a few thousand dollars saved, enough to buy a home and to do something important. But I didn't consider that I wouldn't be able to save everything I made. I'd have to live and spend some of my money. I stood and looked out of the window. I could see the glow of the city lights from this small apartment. I also knew that I didn't want to leave right away. The electrifying city, one I'd never see again once I returned to Argentina, had everything a man needed to succeed. My future lay out there, somewhere, waiting for me to catch up with it. And to do that, I needed more time.

What if . . . what if I didn't wait to marry Luisa until I returned to Argentina? What if I brought her here, and we moved toward our future together? Would she come? My heart picked up speed like when I drank one too many Coca-Colas. Why wouldn't she? What did she have in Argentina? A lousy job? Her family, of course, but I was her future, not her sisters. She had no parents; they'd both died when she was a young girl, so no one could tell her she couldn't come.

I immediately sat down at a small desk and pulled out a sheet of paper to write her a letter. I proposed all over again, but this was a different kind of proposal. I poured my heart out, my words of love and adoration, my desire to build a future together, the promises of adventure and excitement. I told her how much I needed her, that I couldn't survive in this big city alone. Man is not meant to be alone. Someone important said that. God, of course, though I don't believe in God. The author of the bible, then. Either way, it was true. I was lonely. And living in someone else's home, how was this different than living with my parents?

I needed to get my own place. A place for Luisa and me. I needed to be the one in charge of my destiny. I finished the letter, signed it, and placed it in an envelope.

Dropping into bed with my hands behind my head, I stared at the ceiling, excited, imagining that she'd say yes, believing that she would because we loved each other and were meant to live our lives together.

Also by Julia Amante

That Was Then

This Is Now

Let Us Begin

Watch for more at Julia Amante's site.

Praise for Julia Amante's Previous Novels

Let Us Begin

"Julia's best work as she writes the oh-so-familiar drama
of immigration with a special twist. She shows her mettle
as a storyteller with her heart in her hands and poignant
memories that serve to reinforce the challenges and drama
immigrants face even today."

—Nora de Hoyos Comstock, Ph.D. Las Comadres Para
Las Americas

"A moving and thought-provoking book called Let Us Begin describes the difficulties that immigrants face while trying to build a better life for themselves. It explores themes of sacrifice, resiliency, and the unfulfilled promises of the American dream while capturing the essence of the immigrant experience. Readers are compelled to consider the complexities of individual ambition and the true cost of success through Salvador's journey."

—TheLatinoAuthor.com

"Julia Amante's Let Us Begin is a bittersweet exploration of one man's pursuit of the American dream. Love, loyalty and loss are Salvador's companions on his journey from his family home Argentina, as a lonely immigrant in New York, and finally to California where he settles into an imperfect life of his own making. Let Us Begin is a compelling novel that is written with honesty and compassion."

—Margo Candela, Author of The Neapolitan Sisters

"In the pages of this book, you can feel the ups and downs in the life of a man who is in search of opportunity, is willing to take chances, and in the process runs into the hard realities of living away from home."

—Delila Alvarez Vasquez, Producer and Co-Host of
Cafecito Con Podcast

Evenings at the Argentine Club

"A story of family, culture, class, success, and love."
—Booklist

"A big, beautiful novel of love, family, and the close-knit community they inhabit. By turns touching, funny, tragic, and triumphant, it's the story of an endearing group of people in search of their own American dream."
—Susan Wiggs, New York Times bestselling author

"Julia Amante understands the ties that bind all families regardless of culture and nationality—the struggle for identity, the importance of dream, and above all, love. I truly enjoyed Evenings at the Argentine Club."
—Jill Marie Landis, New York Times bestselling author

Say You'll Be Mine

"A gorgeous romance . . . A compelling search for one woman's search for her identity and of what it means to fall in love just as you're discovering who you are."
—Michelle Buonfiglio, Romance B(u)y the Book

"[Amante's] characters are sweetly written and complex...[she] writes them with insight..and explores the moderating line where each individual lives, neither good nor bad, but only human."

—RT Book Reviews

This Is Now

"A compelling and emotional journey about three women dealing with life, love, and loss."

—Caridad Pineiro, Author of The Family She Never Met

About the author

JULIA AMANTE

W omen's Fiction author of *Let Us Begin, This Is Now, That Was Then, Say You'll Be Mine,* and *Evenings at the Argentine Club,* Julia Amante writes emotionally rich stories about family, love, and the passion of chasing and achieving one's goals.

Julia began her writing career in 2000, writing Latina romance under the pseudonym, Lara Rios when Kensington Publishing released a new line of Latino romance books. These books reflected the flavor and rhythm of Latino communities in the U.S. and delivered richly textured commercial fiction about a population that had been mostly ignored by publishers at the time. Julia sold four romances to this publisher before moving on to write longer Chick Lit novels for Berkley Publishing by 2006. Her book *Becoming Latina in 10 Easy Steps* was optioned by Disney's ABC Family to become a future TV series.

In 2009, Lara Rios became Julia Amante when she changed her writing style to reach a new audience. Amante wanted to expand her writing to include not only romantic relationships but the more complex bonds women have with parents, children, and friends. These novels continued to feature Latino characters and the cultural flavor of Hispanic life in America, but they also dealt with universal issues that appealed to women of all cultures.

Julia learned to value her roots and to be proud of her Latina heritage, as well as to be grateful for the life her parents built in the U.S. The beauty of America is that both cultures can be interwoven together, and Julia illustrates this in her novels. To her, being Latina is not separate from being American; her immigrant story is part of the great history of this country.

Julia's other passion is education. She received her B.A. at the University of California, Riverside, and her M.F.A in Fiction from California State University, San Bernardino. She currently teaches writing at California State University, San Bernardino.